LASSOING A MONTANA HEART

RAMONA FLIGHTNER

GRIZZLY DAMSEL PUBLISHING

CHAPTER 1

Bear Grass Springs, Montana Territory; January 1889

Slims never expected to have his world turned upside down on a routine ride to town. The day had begun like any other. Caring for the animals. Mucking out stalls. And then readying the sleigh for the ride into town for supplies, as it appeared the good weather would hold long enough for him and his best friend, Shorty, to make it there and back before the next snowstorm hit.

With the sleigh skidding along a thick pile of snow, Slims sat crammed beside Shorty as they drove toward town on a frigid, clear early January day in Montana Territory. As they slid again around a curve near the sawmill on the outskirts of town, Slims saw Leena Johansen, waving her arm from her front porch. "Whoa!" Slims called out to the fine pair of horses, pulling on the reins to bring them to a smooth halt. "What's the matter, Mrs. Johansen?" he called out.

Leena lived in a fine house near the sawmill—which her husband, Karl, and her brother, Nathanial Ericson, owned outside of the town of Bear Grass Springs. She also worked part-time at the bakery in town with Annabelle MacKinnon. In the nearby distance, he could see the steam rising from the sawmill chimney, indicating her brother and her husband were busy at work.

"Do you need a ride into town?" Slims asked with a deferential nod.

"Is Mette ill?" Shorty asked, inquiring after her young daughter, who was about eighteen months old.

"No, I need your help. Come inside, please," she said, as she smiled at them, her blond hair tied back in an elaborate braid and her blue eyes shining with worry. Although she spoke English well, she still had an accent from her native Norway.

Slims and Shorty shared a long look but did not argue. Slims set the brake, tossing the reins to Shorty to tie them up. Slims pulled out two blankets to cover the horses, stretching as he worked. He followed Shorty up the steps and into the warm house, sighing with pleasure at the delicious scents wafting around him. Closing his eyes, he breathed deeply. "It smells like heaven in here."

"*Ja*," Leena said with a giggle. "That's what my Karl always says to me." She now held her daughter in her arms, shifting from foot to foot to keep Mette calm. Leena glanced at the kitchen table. "I made cookies today. Please have one or two."

Slims shared another look with Shorty, before snatching up a gingerbread cookie. "Truly heaven, missus," he mumbled. After taking another bite, he asked, "What is the matter? What has you worried?"

Leena nodded in the direction of the corner behind the door. "I don't know what to do with her."

Slims spun and dropped the remainder of his cookie to the floor. "Ma'am—miss—ma'am," he stuttered out.

The woman in the corner had hair so blond that it seemed as pale as sunlight, her smooth ivory complexion highlighted by a smattering of freckles on her nose, with an air of fragility about her. She stood a little taller than Shorty's five feet and clutched a jacket around her, as though embarrassed or ashamed.

"I beg your pardon." He tapped Shorty on his arm, but he merely grunted. Holding a hand out to her, as he did whenever he attempted to calm a skittish horse, Slims murmured, "You're safe, miss."

"I dinna ken where to go," she whispered.

"You're Scottish," Shorty exclaimed. "Like Sorcha."

At Sorcha's name, she edged toward them. "Aye." She took a deep breath. "I was trying to reach a woman named Sorcha …" She paused and closed her eyes, as though recalling a name. "MacKinnon."

"She's not a MacKinnon no longer," Shorty said with a friendly smile. "She's a Tompkins now. An' she lives out at the Mountain Bluebird Ranch. Where we work." He pointed at himself and Slims.

The unknown woman took a step from the shadows, and Slims caught his breath at the desperation in her gaze. "You'll be well, ma'am. Miss." He swore softly for acting like a tongue-tied teenager. "If you're a friend of Sorcha's, we will bring you to the ranch. We'll ensure nothing happens to you."

She stared at them, a fine quivering moving through her body. "I dinna ken how I can trust you."

"You've made it this far from Scotland," Slims soothed. "The ranch isn't but a short distance from here."

Leena took a step forward, her blue eyes shining with curiosity. "Are you the new cook they're waiting for?"

The woman met their expectant gazes, slowly shaking her head. "Nae," she whispered. "Nae, I'm Sorcha's cousin, Davina MacQueen. Come to meet her at last."

～

3

Davina forced herself to move away from the corner of the room, determined not to cower like a recalcitrant schoolgirl. *I'm almost forty!* she silently chided herself. However, the man towering over a foot taller than her, with a muscular barrel chest, rendered her nearly speechless. His brown eyes appeared to gleam with concern, but she had learned caution was truly the better part of valor on her long journey from Scotland. Or was it discretion? She never could remember her schoolbooks with any accuracy.

Her gaze skirted to Leena, the kind woman who had insisted she rest inside as she trudged past her house on the snow-covered road. Leena appeared at ease with the incongruous duo—the giant of a man and the tiny man beside him, who looked almost dwarflike in comparison. "What are yer names?" she whispered.

"I'm Slims, and he's Shorty," the giant responded.

Unable to fight a giggle, she covered her mouth to stifle her inappropriate reaction in her hope that she wouldn't offend them.

Slims nodded at her humor, not offended in any way by her reaction. "Yes, that's how most respond. They also call us the Giant and the Dwarf." He shrugged. "We far prefer our own nicknames."

"Who gave them to ye?" she asked, her widened eyes filled with curiosity.

Slims shared an amused glance with the man who seemed a good friend, and he shrugged. "The latter names were given to us by a man who's one of the greatest rascals I've ever met." He paused, as a fondness flit over his expression. "And a fine man. Harold Tompkins. If you spend any time at the ranch, I'm sure you'll meet him. He's grandfather to Sorcha's husband."

Davina sobered, as she focused again on why she was

here. "Aye, my cousin," she breathed. "I was walkin' to her home, but Mrs. Johansen feared I would lose my way."

Shorty stepped up to stand beside Slims, with his hands on his hips and his eyes flashing. "Walkin' in the middle of winter from town? Are you mad, woman?" He grunted when Slims belted him on his chest. "I beg your pardon. I shouldn't speak to the boss's family like that."

Davina lost her battle with her smile and grinned at the two men. "I fear I'm actin' like a fool, but you both seem harmless enough." She watched as the giant choked at her word choice.

"If you mean, we won't attempt any mischief with you, ma'am, you are correct," he said, although she reminded him of Sorcha with her show of spirit. "However, let me assure you that we are far from harmless."

She watched as the two men turned away from her in a huff to speak to the kind woman who had given Davina shelter for a few hours. She saw the giant, who called himself Slims, pick up the piece of cookie that had fallen and offer to sweep the floor. She watched the men converse with Leena for a moment, realizing they were acquaintances, if not friends, and Davina felt out of place, as she was not included in the conversation.

Embarrassed, she rubbed one damp sock over her opposite ankle as she belatedly remembered her boots were by the stove. Hoping to move without garnering any notice, she slunk in the direction of the stove, stilling when she saw Slims watching her. She flushed and then shrugged, continuing her quest to don her boots.

She tugged one on, but the second boot wasn't as dry as the first. When her foot got stuck halfway into the boot, she slammed her foot down, in an attempt to force the boot in place. Rather than helping her, she lost her balance and careened to the side. Gasping with shock, she looked up to

5

see Slims cradling her against his chest, as he prevented her from falling to the floor. "I dinna ken what happened," she gasped.

Davina's gasp turned into a sputter as Slims quickly knelt, and his strong hands tugged on her sock and boot, easing her foot into place.

"Don't worry, ma'am," Slims said with a wry smile. "Your cousin is a walking calamity too. Besides, you know I'm harmless." He nodded to her in a deferential manner that also managed to be insolent, before turning to the door to exit the house.

Davina shared a long look with Leena. "Thank ye for yer kindness, Mrs. Johansen." She pulled her cloak around her as she moved to follow the men outside.

Leena set a hand on Davina's arm. "Any family of Sorcha's is always welcome here," she said with a smile, her gaze on the retreating backs of the ranch hands. "Don't worry about them. They're men, and they are offended by the smallest things." She winked at Davina. "Tell Sorcha that I'd love for her to visit when next the weather is clear."

Davina nodded and followed the men to the sleigh, pausing to note the sleigh's size. "Do ye no' think it would be better for me to walk?" she called out. She heard the men sigh with disgust and mutter the word "harmless" again as she approached them. "There is no' room for more than two on the seat."

Slims paused in patting the horses and praising them. "Where is your trunk? Your possessions?" He stared at her as she shrugged. "Come. Shorty will ride in the back, and you can sit beside me. We'll have to share a blanket so Shorty can have one too." He motioned her to him and eased her into the sleigh, wrapping the blanket tight around her.

The sleigh heaved a little as Shorty hopped in the back, and then Slims got in beside her. "Sit behind her, Short!" he called out. When they were ready, he made a fine clicking noise and ably turned the sleigh around. With a final wave to Leena holding Mette, they sped away from the house on the edge of town.

"I dinna think to ask why ye were about today," she murmured.

"About?" Slims asked. "Oh, you mean, what we were doing." He shrugged. "We had hoped to go into town for supplies. Perhaps we'll go in tomorrow, if the weather remains clear."

"Turn around, Mr. Slims. Ye can no' change yer plans simply for me," she protested, tugging on his large arm, although it felt as though she were yanking on an oak trunk and just as immobile. She gave a grunt of frustration as the sleigh continued on its forward progression in the opposite direction from town. "Sir," she said in a serious tone that only elicited a chuckle.

"If that's what you sound like when you're mad, you'll never get anyone to do your biddin', ma'am," he said with a smile, as he peered down at her. "You sound like a disgruntled kitten."

"Perhaps, but kittens have claws, aye?" she snapped, crossing her arms over her chest, as she huffed out a breath of air, causing a puff of white to emerge in front of her.

Rather than attempt any more conversation with the infuriating man, she thought about her long journey from Scotland. The harrowing carriage ride through the glens as she fled to Glasgow and its nearby port. The seemingly never-ending ocean crossing, where she had wished at times she would die rather than suffer any more seasickness. The ever-present fear that her name would not confer her the deference she desired, as men stared at her with lascivious interest. And the constant worry that her coins would run out.

7

Upon landing in America, she realized her name meant little here, and none would proffer their respect due to a fear of retribution. Ever since she had arrived, a wariness had seeped into her very marrow, and she feared what would happen if she let her guard down for one moment. Even sleeping on the train left her vulnerable, although the conductors had worked to ensure she was undisturbed during the long journey west. Finally, after months of travel, she had reached Bear Grass Springs, unable to quell the ache in her heart for her homeland. Feeling fanciful, she gave silent thanks to the Fairy Queen for ensuring she arrived unharmed.

Banishing her thoughts about her difficult journey, she focused on the scenery around her. All during the long train ride west, she had thought nothing could compare to the beauty of the Isle of Skye in Scotland. The place she had always called home. However, as she looked up and glanced at the mountains, fresh snow gleaming on their peaks, the sun beaming down on them so they glistened, her breath caught. Perhaps she had been wrong. For here was a place that could rival her beloved home.

A cloudless blue sky overhead seemed to accentuate the pristine white of the snow blanketing the valley floor. Bushes formed an ambling path in the valley floor, as though following a frozen-over creek. In the distance, a few houses were visible, their plumes of smoke rising into the sky from chimneys. As she glanced at the mountains again, she saw an area void of trees from peak to valley floor, as though brushed free by a painter.

"What happened to that part of the mountain?" she asked, as she pointed to the distant mountain.

Slims squinted in the bright sunlight in that direction. "Avalanche."

She gazed at him with a disgruntled expression for his

curt response. "Why is this land empty?" she asked, unable to fight her curiosity and to keep her questions to herself.

"It's good grazing land in the spring and summer," Slims said. "Although we try to keep the cattle closer to home now, after the bad winter we had a few years ago."

She shook her head in bewilderment but didn't ask any more questions. She relaxed under the blanket, subtly trying to huddle closer to his warmth. When Slims spoke, she stiffened.

"Miss Sorcha never said she was expectin' you," he said with a glance in her direction.

"*Ach*, well, that could be because I never wrote to tell her that I was comin'," Davina said, her gaze on the distant mountains. "I thought I'd surprise her."

An uncomfortable silence settled between them as the horses sped down the road, before turning onto a smaller road upon reaching the sign noting Mountain Bluebird Ranch. She fought an unease that soon she would meet her cousin, gripping her hands together tightly on her lap. Silently she prayed her cousin was nothing like her da. For, if Sorcha were like him, Davina would have nowhere to go. She shivered at the thought of being stranded in the middle of Montana Territory in winter.

As Slims expertly brought the horses to a halt in front of the ranch house, he murmured to her, "A word of caution, ma'am. None here like deceit." He hopped out and offered her a hand down.

≈

As his name was called, Slims turned toward the barn, where they stalled the horses. With a muttered, "Wait here," to Davina, he walked toward his boss, Frederick Tompkins. "Boss," he muttered.

9

"What are you doing back here so quickly? Was there trouble in town?" Frederick's alert gaze looked over Slims's shoulder, and he frowned at the sight of Davina. "Who's the woman?"

"She claims she's Miss Sorcha's cousin, come from Scotland," Slims said in a low voice. "She had walked as far as the sawmill before Mrs. Johansen made her come inside." He kicked at a frozen piece of dirt. "We never got far enough to town to get supplies."

Frederick waved away the concern about supplies, his gaze wholly focused on the newcomer. "Relation or not, I won't have her upsetting Sorcha," Frederick muttered, as he walked toward the woman. Frederick was the youngest of the Tompkins brothers and spent the entire year on the ranch, running it. His two older brothers, Peter and Cole, traveled to Texas to drive a herd north each year, although every year they said it would be the last time they attempted the journey.

A handsome man, Frederick stood inches shorter than Slims. He had always charmed women but had never been truly charmed himself until Sorcha MacKinnon had won his heart. Now there wasn't anything he wouldn't do to keep her happy. As he approached the unknown woman, Slims noted that Boss pasted on an impersonal smile, outwardly friendly, but with an undercurrent of unease.

Rather than help Shorty unhitch the horses and rub them down, Slims stood behind Frederick, watching the interaction between his boss and Davina MacQueen. Unwillingly, Davina fascinated Slims. Her bursts of bravado wedded to an air of fragility acted as a siren's call for him. One he feared he'd have trouble ignoring, if she were to remain for long on the ranch.

He watched as Davina's astute gaze roved over Frederick, taking in his tall broad-shouldered frame, as he loomed over her. Frederick's black hair blew in the gentle breeze, and Slims moved to the side to see his piercing blue eyes wholly focused on the woman.

"I'm Frederick, and, for your purposes, I own the ranch." He paused, as though seeing if she would react to his words. When she continued to stare at him innocently, he sighed. "Why are you here?"

Davina's gaze flickered to Slims a moment and then back to Frederick. "I was told yer wife was Sorcha MacKinnon. She's my cousin."

Frederick relaxed a little at the unmistakable Scottish accent, so similar to his wife's. "Aye, she's my wife. Where in Scotland are you from?"

"The town of Portree, on the Isle of Skye," she said, glancing to the mountains in the distance. "Never did I think to find mountains to rival the Cuillin's. I doubt ye have fairies here, aye?"

Frederick laughed. "Depends on your definition of fairies." He smiled and motioned for her to follow him. "Come. I'll introduce you to Sorcha. Slims, why don't you join us?"

Slims nodded, a battle raging inside him. Part of him hoped Davina would be proven a fraud and forced to leave the ranch. The part he did not want to acknowledge hoped that she was truly Sorcha's cousin and that he would have a reason to see her. Every day. He sighed, for he feared he had just lost his mind.

∽

Davina followed the cautious, yet reluctantly friendly man called Frederick into the large house. Fighting trepidation at her cousin's reaction to her precipitous arrival, Davina held her shoulders back and her head high, pasting on a calm expression. She saw Slims stare at her curiously as she passed him, but she ignored his mocking smirk.

After ascending the steps and crossing the threshold to the house, she fought a sigh of relief to enter a warm space. Even Leena's home hadn't been this warm. Glancing around the large living area, Davina saw a fireplace on one wall, with crackling wood burning within. She battled the urge to approach it to warm her hands and feet. Instead she stood demurely by the door. A soft singing could be heard from a room down a long hallway, a song Davina recognized from her childhood.

"Come. Be comfortable," Frederick murmured, as he motioned for her to sit by the fire.

She watched Frederick walk down the hallway before she sat on a settee. She tried to act nonchalant as she squirmed her feet closer to the fire, but she saw Slims staring at her with an amused gleam in his gaze and knew she had failed. "My feet are still wet," she muttered with a flush.

"I imagine they are, ma'am. When things are settled, you'll be shown to a room and can freshen up." He frowned again. "Although I didn't retrieve your trunk. Where is it?"

Davina sighed. "It was too heavy to tug after me. I left it at the station. The stationmaster said he'd look after it for a day or two."

Slims swore under his breath. "You'd better hope the weather holds. If it doesn't, there'll be nothing left but the trunk when we return." He shrugged. "He'll see it as abandoned property after a few days and sell the contents for profit. It's how he augments his meager wage."

Davina's eyes rounded with shock. "I thought he'd act more honorably."

Slims shrugged again. "You did leave it behind. And honor is all a matter of perspective."

"'Twas too heavy!" She stomped her foot, looking at him

as though she wished she could stomp on his. "Ye ken as well as I that I couldna have dragged a trunk in the snow."

Slims fought a chuckle at her indignation. "No, but you could have waited. Or spoken with someone. The MacKinnons are a welcoming family. They would have aided you."

"I'm *bluidy* tired of needin' aid," she muttered, crossing her arms over her chest.

Crouching to be at her eye level, Slims watched her closely. "Oh, but that's exactly where you are, ma'am. You're here, needin' Boss's and Miss Sorcha's aid. Because you claim to be her long-lost cousin come to call. It makes me wonder why you were so eager to leave a little town like Bear Grass Springs behind with such haste. What are you running from?" He paused as he stared for a long moment into her tormented brown eyes. "Or who?"

"Slims, leave her be," a woman called out.

"Miss Sorcha," Slims said, as he rose, his voice filled with warmth and affection, as he stood between the two women. "I meant no harm."

Sorcha chuckled as she ran a hand down his strong arm. "Aye, but ye ken what it is like to be among strangers for the first time. It can muddle yer wits and scare ye, so ye dinna ken what's up nor down, aye?"

"Aye," the big man said with a smile. He stepped back, allowing Sorcha to stand in front of Davina.

Sorcha Tompkins was a short woman, barely over five feet tall. However, she had a strength of will and a matching personality that ensured all near her eagerly followed her every wish, even the giant of a man standing beside her. Her husband, Frederick, had teased her that it was because she was part Fairy Queen, but he and all the men of the ranch knew it was due to her compassion, her constancy, and her consideration for others that they felt an overwhelming loyalty and love for her. Her red-brown hair shone more red than brown as she stood in front of the fire, and the sky-blue wool of her dress enhanced the natural beauty of her blue eyes.

Her inquisitive gaze looked over Davina with a frown. "Ye dinna look like any cousin I ever met. Ye canna be a MacKinnon." She frowned as she motioned for Davina to stand up.

Davina rose, standing slightly taller than Sorcha, her blond hair falling loose from its pins and cascading down her back.

"Ah, 'tis beautiful," Sorcha whispered. "As are ye, Miss ... ?"

"I was born a MacQueen," Davina breathed, so nervous she could barely speak. She pulled and pushed at her hair until she had knotted it at her nape again.

"*MacQueen*," Sorcha rasped, stumbling. She murmured her thanks, as Slims reached forward to grab her arm, ensuring she didn't fall. "I didna ken any MacQueen was willin' to acknowledge me."

"I'm Davina. My da is Baldwin MacQueen, the patriarch of the family and your uncle." She paused as though uncertain if she should say more. After another hesitation, she blurted out, "Your mother's brother."

"Aye, Mairi's," Sorcha said.

Davina heaved out a deep breath, as though her tension left with it. "You know about Mairi?"

Sorcha made a motion for Davina to sit and nodded to Slims, who left the room. She sat on the settee, facing Davina, Frederick standing behind her, his steady hand on her shoulder, as Sorcha grasped his hand and squeezed it. "Aye, another man who claimed to be brother to my mother visited me afore I left Scotland and told me about her. I never kent her."

Davina frowned. "That must have been Uncle Fergus. He's always enjoyed goin' against Da's commands."

"Why are you here?" Frederick asked.

Sorcha made a sound of disgust in her throat. "Too direct, love," she murmured. "The Scots prefer a roundabout way of approachin' things."

He rolled his eyes and sighed as he settled onto the settee, urging Sorcha to lean against him. "As long as we know what's going on by the time the twins wake up."

Davina looked at the two of them and smiled. "Twins?" she whispered. "You have twins?"

"Aye, a boy and a girl," Sorcha said, unable to hide the pride in her voice. "Wee Harold and Mairi."

Davina made a soft sound of surprise. "Oh, how beautiful. You named her after your mother. She would have loved that."

Sorcha sat up, leaning forward urgently. "You knew my mother?" At Davina's nod, she looked at Frederick. "She knew my mother."

"*Shh*, it's all right, Sorcha," he whispered, as he traced away a tear that flowed down her cheek.

Davina sat in wonder as she watched the couple, their love for each other starkly evident in the way he cared for her and her trust in turning to him. Davina battled envy and regret to never have known such devotion in her life. She feared she never would.

Frederick cleared his voice, interrupting her thoughts. "As I was reprimanded, I know I am acting inappropriately. However, why are you here? You're upsetting my wife, and I'd like to know why."

Davina froze. She watched as Slims returned with a tray filled with mismatched cups and plates, a teapot, and a cake to slice up, which he left on a nearby table. He pulled out a chair and sat, watching them. In that instant, she felt as though she were on trial. "I had thought Sorcha dead," Davina whispered. "That is the story Da told us, ever since I was a girl, ten years old and mournin' the death of my favorite aunt Mairi and the child she was to have." She looked at Sorcha. "I had hoped to have a girl cousin. I'd only had brothers and boy cousins."

Sorcha's breath caught on a sob.

"For years, I believed the lie. Until I was pushed into a corner and desperate. I ransacked my da's private library and found correspondence that proved ye had lived. Ye hadna died with my beloved auntie." She closed her eyes. "And I no longer kent what to believe. Who to believe. I was lost."

"So you traveled to America?" Slims asked with a shake of his head. "Seems a drastic measure to take when you could have written a letter."

She half laughed, half sobbed, as she covered her mouth a moment. "Aye, I ken. But I couldna be forced into a loveless marriage. No' by a man who had shown such disloyalty to his sister. How could I believe my da's reassurances that he'd ensured my well-bein' in the marriage contracts when I kent him to be a liar?" Davina shook her head. "I couldna risk a life of misery. I couldna. So I ran. An' I ran. An' I'm here."

"Oh, Davina," Sorcha whispered, as she eased from Frederick's hold to move to her cousin. "Oh, I'm so sorry for how you suffered." She wrapped an arm around her cousin's shoulders. "I wish … I wish I could have done somethin' more for ye before now."

Davina sat with shoulders stooped and battling sobs. "I'm sorry for appearin' unwanted on yer doorstep."

Laughing, Sorcha pulled her cousin into a tight hug. "Oh, ye wee daft woman, if there's one thing we MacKinnons yearn for, 'tis more family." She held Davina as a sob burst out, holding her close. "*Shh*, cousin, ye're safe now."

∿

S lims strode into the barn to find Dalton currying horses. He heard Shorty talking with the youngest ranch hand, Dixon, in the tack room, and Slims approached Dalton. After grabbing a brush, Slims began to work on a horse. During the long winter months, only the four of them remained at the ranch to keep it running, along with Frederick. Many more men arrived in the spring to work the spring-to-fall seasons, hoping to earn enough to survive until the following year. Slims knew that he, Shorty, Dalton, and Dixon considered themselves the most fortunate of men to have year-round employment on a ranch with employers who were like family.

"What's she like?" Dalton asked. He stood a few inches shorter than six feet, with a wiry frame. His brown hair was longer than usual in midwinter without a recent haircut, and his blue eyes glinted with curiosity.

"Feisty, like her cousin," Slims muttered. When he brushed too hard on the chestnut filly's hindquarters, and she shifted her legs, he murmured soothing words to her. "Easy."

Dalton leaned against one of the barn's poles, tossing his brush from hand to hand as he studied his boss. "Seems to me that she'll liven things up on this ranch this winter. It's been mighty boring." When Slims did little more than grunt his agreement, Dalton laughed. "Well, Shorty said she wasn't for him, and Dix is too young for her, so it seems I might have a chance at a new bride." His gaze turned distant, as though remembering his wife, Mary, who had died three years ago in childbirth.

"You'd never know a moment's peace," Slims said, as he stepped out of the stall. "She's impetuous. Traveling all the way from Scotland, not even knowin' if she would be welcomed here. And she's a determined one. Thought she would walk here from the train station."

17

Dalton stilled as he watched his friend and foreman. "Oh, I see."

Staring at his friend, Slims shook his head, as he attempted to step past him. "There's nothin' to see. The woman interrupted our trip to town, and now we have to wait for the weather to clear again. Another storm's blowin' in as we speak."

Dalton stepped in front of him, stopping his huge friend from sidling past. "No, Slims. I remember well the winter Sorcha came to us. The winter we nearly lost it all." He waited as Slims stood tall, breathing hard, although he'd hardly exerted himself. Dalton watched his friend closely, and he suspected it had nothing to do with the memories of the harsh winter where a warm day was twenty below zero and when they could do nothing more than pray that the cattle would survive out on the prairie. Instead he suspected Slims's agitation had everything to do with the new arrival. "I remember you saying the only woman who would ever interest you, could ever interest you, would be Sorcha MacKinnon's cousin." Dalton grinned. "Well, it seems she's finally come callin'."

"Fool," Slims snapped, as he stormed past Dalton. Slims ignored Dalton's chuckle, moving to the water pump to fill buckets of water to bring to the horses. Although this was work usually completed by Dixon, Slims needed the physical distraction, and he planned on mucking out stalls, either here or in the other barn. Anything to take his mind off the new arrival.

A few hours later, he paused, as he pitched hay into a stall for their milk cows. Leaning on the pitchfork, he stared back at the peaceful, contented face of the Jersey cow, named Sunset for its rich gold coat. He leaned forward and patted it on its side. "You don't have any concerns, do you, girl?" He sighed when he heard a chuckle.

"Seems the woman's already been successful if she's drivin' you to talk to Sunset," Shorty said, as he joined him.

Slims set aside his pitchfork and stood staring into the darkened interior of the secondary barn that held the pigs, goats, and milk cows. It wasn't as grand a space as the large barn that housed the horses, but it had a more intimate feel. "She's the boss's cousin. And I'm too old for any woman."

Shorty belted him in his arm, as though that would knock sense into him. "You barely know the woman. Perhaps she's an *imposer*." He ignored Slims's muttered comment, "*Imposter*," correcting his misspoken word. "Perhaps she's stark raving mad. You shouldn't be this tied up in knots after only spending a few minutes in her company."

Slims shrugged, his vision filled with the memory of her blond hair falling free of its pins and cascading down her back. Oh, how his fingers had itched to run through those silky strands. How he wished he had the right to do it. Shaking his head and heaving out a deep breath, he pushed aside such fantasies. He shared a rueful smile with his best friend and shrugged once more. "You know what a longing does to a man's soul, Shorty."

"Yes, but you don't know if she's worth havin' a hankerin' for. Give it time, Slims." He paused before saying in a soft voice, "You don't want to make the same mistake as ..."

Slims stilled and shook his head. Any infatuation had been replaced by a steely cold resolve at the reminder of his past transgressions. "No. But I might have already committed the gravest sin, Short. I delivered her here, and they've welcomed her in. If anything were to happen to Frederick, Miss Sorcha, or the little ones ..." He let out a deep breath, as he refused to relive the tragedy that had struck the last time he had trusted a woman.

CHAPTER 2

Upon awakening, Davina had found dresses and underclothes on the chair beside the bed, along with towels and fresh water in the ewer on the bureau. Although the clothes weren't a perfect fit, they were close enough, and she was grateful for her cousin's kindness. After washing up a bit and changing into new clothes, Davina had ventured downstairs to the living room, uncertain if she should seek out her cousin.

Having slept through supper, Davina was surprised a plate of food had been saved for her in the warming oven. However, Sorcha had acted as though it were normal behavior to set aside food for someone who had missed a meal.

Now Davina rested on the settee in the living room near the fireplace, gazing into the flames, her thoughts a jumbled mess. She had never thought to be so unhesitatingly accepted by her cousin. Davina fought a sinking sense of shame that she would not have so readily taken in Sorcha had she arrived on Davina's doorstep, destitute and desperate for aid.

With a deep sigh, Davina attempted to calm her racing

thoughts, forcing herself to think about the beautiful scenery she had passed during the sleigh ride to the ranch. However, her mind wandered to consider the man who had so easily managed the horses, and she struggled to forget him.

"Was the man so horrible?" Sorcha asked in a quiet voice. She sat beside her cousin, her knitting needles *clack*ing, as the fire crackled in front of them. Meanwhile Frederick could be heard muttering in his nearby office.

Davina gave a small jolt, out of her memories and back to the present. "Nae," she whispered. She met her cousin's patient gaze with a hint of curiosity and shook her head. "Nae," she whispered again.

Sorcha calmly watched her, waiting to see if Davina would say more.

"He never seemed upset that he had to return to the ranch with me."

Sorcha giggled, a light flush coloring her complexion and the firelight making her seem even younger than her twenty-eight years. "Nae, no' Slims. The man in Skye."

Davina's eyes widened, and she blushed with mortification at her misunderstanding of her cousin. "Oh," she whispered, her gaze dropping to her fingers, clenched together on her lap. "He was a good man. A kind man. A nice man."

Sorcha's needles stilled, as she thought through what Davina refrained from saying. "Borin' as watchin' a kettle, waitin' for it to boil?" Sorcha said with a wry smile. When Davina flushed, Sorcha chuckled. "Why would your da want ye to marry him?"

Playing with a loose thread on her skirt, Davina shrugged. "My da, your uncle, is a businessman, and I was a means to ensure the business prospered. My future sons were to strengthen the claim we had as the most important family in Portree. I ken that doesna seem important here, but, on Skye, it is." Davina's gaze was distant. "Da never saw me as anythin' other than a woman who owed him my fealty. He never cared what I wanted."

At the long silence, where a low wind howled outside, Sorcha murmured, "And? What 'tis it ye desire?"

"Love," Davina said. "A man to want me, no' because I'm a MacQueen or because my da is powerful. But because the man wants me." Her eyes gleamed with passionate sincerity. "It's no' too much to ask, is it?"

"No," Sorcha said with a smile. "When ye meet the rest of the family, ye'll see we've all married for love."

Davina sighed, some of her tension leaving her. "I've never kent that. My mother married my da because her da told her to. Theirs was a practical marriage, an' they dinna understand my desire for more. My da only saw me as a woman who had to do his bidding because I'd be destitute without him."

"Ye are no'," Sorcha said, her needles clattering together as she made a disgusted sound in the back of her throat. "Ye have family, and, although we ken lean times on the ranch, ye will never starve."

"Thank ye," Davina said. "Although I know I must find a way to be useful. I'd hate to be a burden."

Sorcha smiled. "This is a workin' ranch. There's always plenty to do an' I'm certain ye'll find somethin' ye enjoy." With a sly smile, she said, "Or at least tolerate." After minutes where the only sounds were again of the fire crackling and her needles *click*ing together, she said, "'Tis interestin' ye should have noticed Slims."

Davina rested her head against the back of the settee, her eyes closed, as though soaking in the warmth from the fire. "He'd be a hard man to ignore." She flushed beet red at her cousin's chortle. "Do no' get ideas of matchmakin'," Davina warned, as she turned her head to meet her cousin's innocent gaze. "I did no' race halfway across the world to escape my da's wily ways to run into yers."

Sorcha sobered. "Of course no'," she murmured. "Forgive me for teasin' ye." She continued to watch her cousin through her lowered gaze. She frowned as Davina played with one of her fingers, as though caressing a ring no longer present. "Ye were married afore," she whispered, her brows furrowed, as though in absolute befuddlement.

Davina stilled the motion of her fingers, flushing beet red. Her gaze rose to Sorcha's, her brown eyes lit with panic as Sorcha watched her with curiosity. "Aye," Davina whispered. "To a MacDonald."

Sorcha goggled at the news her cousin had been married into one of the most powerful families on Skye. "A MacDonald? An' who were ye to marry the second time?"

"A MacDonald cousin," she whispered. "They joked I would no' have to worry about rememberin' a new name." Davina closed her eyes and ducked her head, as though in shame.

Setting aside her needles, Sorcha scooted closer to her cousin. She clasped Davina's hand, giving it a gentle squeeze. "Come. It canna be as bad as all that." She smiled as Davina appeared to relax in front of her. "Ye're here, in Montana." Her smile broadened at the thought. "Ye must have been terrified of the man to have raced away."

Davina shook her head. "Nae," she whispered. "I wanted a taste of freedom is all."

Sorcha rested her head against the back of the settee, curling up on it as she studied her cousin. "If ye married one MacDonald, ye should already be a bit of an heiress."

Flushing, Davina shrugged. "I have coins sewn into my cape. An' jewels hidden in the hem of my petticoats."

Sorcha burst out laughing. "Oh, 'tis a fine day that you came to call, cousin, on your quest for freedom and love."

When she heard the first cry from one of her twins, she rose with a contented sigh. Resting a hand on Davina's shoulder, Sorcha urged her to remain by the fire. "Rest and warm yerself. I'll return when they are settled again."

Davina watched as Frederick emerged from his office, his hand outstretched to link with Sorcha's, as he murmured something to his wife to cause her to blush and giggle. They walked to the nearby room, where the children slept, and Davina heard the murmur of their voices as they talked to their children.

A heretofore unknown envy filled Davina. She wanted that. She wanted a man so dedicated to her and to their children that he would set aside his work to join his family. She yearned for a man so devoted that he craved time spent with her as much as she did with him.

During her mad dash across the sea and this continent, all she had focused on was her goal of arriving. Her fear at her reception had consumed her. Now that she had reached the ranch and had met her cousin, Davina realized how naive she had been. She had never thought of what she would do or what her life would be away from Portree. She was not a crofter's daughter. She couldn't fathom how a ranch worked. What could she possibly offer them?

"Fool," she muttered to herself, as she rested her head against the back of the settee. She fought her greatest fear: That her da was right. That she was only valued for a liaison she could make for her family. Never for herself alone.

~

Davina slipped into the kitchen the following morning, the scent of bacon, fresh baked bread, and coffee acting like a beacon. Her steps stilled the moment she entered the room at the sight of all four ranch hands seated at the table. "I beg yer pardon," she whispered, her eyes rounded.

Slims stood, and the other men followed suit. She flushed and waved at them to retake their seats. All wore rough work clothes, although they appeared to have washed up before the morning meal.

Sorcha bustled in behind her, absently tucking in strands of loose hair. "Davina, I'm glad ye woke in time for breakfast." She beamed at her. "Ye ken Shorty and Slims," she said, pointing to the two men who sat across from each other at the table, "and this is Dixon and Dalton."

"A pleasure to meet ye," Davina said.

"Ma'am," Dalton said. He kicked Dixon who had been on the verge of rising again.

Sitting with a *thud*, Dixon glared at the older man. "Nice to meet you, missus. Sure is nice to have another pretty woman on the ranch. And to think that you're Miss Sorcha's cousin. Aren't we lucky?"

Sorcha smiled at her cousin before scowling. "Ye ken we're supposed to get another cook. A storm must have delayed her."

Dixon brightened even further. "Then we'll have even more women on the ranch."

"And you'll still be single," Shorty muttered, earning a snicker from Dalton and a grin from Slims.

Frederick entered, pausing to squeeze Sorcha's shoulders and to kiss the back of her head. "Or she's heard about us and came to her senses." He winked at Davina, as he poured himself a cup of coffee from the pot sitting on the stove. "Davina?" he asked, holding up the pot. At her nod, he poured her one too and brought it to the table. He motioned for Davina to sit. Sorcha would sit beside her with Frederick at the head of the table.

Dixon stared with wide-eyed fascination at Davina, who

sat across from him. A strand of blond hair fell into his eyes, and he brushed it away. "Do you cook?"

"Dix," Dalton hissed with another kick to the young cowboy.

Davina looked at everyone watching her with unveiled curiosity. "Aye, I cook a little. But I ken ye would eat better if someone else were preparin' yer meals." She frowned as they all laughed.

Frederick picked up a piece of bacon to chew on. "Slims is on duty tonight, and I know we'd all prefer if we didn't have to eat his hash again." He smiled at his foreman to show he was teasing.

"At least I don't burn down the house when boilin' water, Boss," Slims said with a sly smile.

Frederick and Sorcha blushed beet red at the comment. "Ah, that was an unfortunate event," Frederick stammered out, as he fought an embarrassed chuckle. "My attention was diverted. I thought it was the heat of the moment. Never realized it was heat from another reason." He shrugged as the ranch hands burst out laughing.

"You're lucky you didn't singe more than your favorite pair of pantaloons," Dixon said, his brown eyes glowing with mischief and glee. When he saw Davina staring at them, as though they had gone mad, Dixon laughed and pointed his fork at Frederick. "Boss got a bit too lovey-dovey with Miss Sorcha and had a kitchen disaster."

"Oh my," Davina breathed.

"We're fortunate it was summer, and we saw the smoke comin' out the open window," Shorty said, as he lost his battle with his laughter and began to chortle. "Never did see two people jump apart faster than those two when they realized the near calamity they'd caused."

"And when they had a perfectly good bed upstairs,"

Dalton muttered with a shake of his head, although he grinned broadly.

Davina glanced around the kitchen, which showed no evidence of any near calamity. "Ye'd never ken a near disaster had been had in here."

"Well, most kitchens aren't whitewashed," Frederick said, as he winked at his wife. "Took a few coats to cover up the singe marks." He smiled at Davina. "However, I'm the sly one. I've been off kitchen duty for over six months now."

"Ye have no," Sorcha protested. "Ye still have to do dishes." She laughed. "An' ye ken we dreaded every meal ye prepared."

Davina sat in silent wonder as she watched the ranch hands interact with their boss and the boss's wife. She had never imagined such familiarity between hired hands and the owners of a large establishment like this ranch.

Slims focused on Davina, his brown eyes intense and serious. "So the question remains, miss. Can you cook?" When she paused, he asked, "Will you cook for us?"

Davina cast a furtive glance at the large stove. "I will cook, but I'll need help learnin' how to use that stove. I imagine 'tis different from the ones in Skye."

"Aye," Sorcha said, "'tis. But 'twould be a big help to me. I have yarn to spin and the bairns to tend." She smiled at Slims in an innocent manner. "I'd be most grateful, Slims, if ye'd take the time to teach Davina all ye ken. Ye've prepared plenty of meals on that beast of a stove."

Slims flashed her an irritated look before nodding. "Of course, Miss Sorcha. Whatever you would like." He pushed away from the table, picking up his plate to bring to the sink. "I'll be back this afternoon, miss, to work with you."

Davina nodded, as she watched the other men gobble down the rest of their food and then follow their foreman outside. When the room went silent, too silent she realized, she asked, "Why do they eat here?" She cringed when she saw the disappointment in Sorcha's gaze and then the friendliness fading from Frederick's gaze.

"This is no laird's house," Sorcha snapped, rising to bring her dish to the sink and to begin the cleanup. "We work together and ken each other's problems. We like each other. An', if we dinna like ye, ye dinna stay long." She sighed, as she rubbed at her temples. "Both cooks abandoned us, one in November, the other in December. One to run away to marry a miner. The other to God kens where." She slammed down a pan in frustration.

"Sorch," Frederick said in a calming voice that also held a note of warning.

"I can cook and clean," Davina whispered. "I should do something if ye are lettin' me stay here." She looked from Sorcha to Frederick and back to her cousin. "I did no' mean any criticism. Life here is different from what I ken, aye?"

Sorcha stilled her frenetic movements and set aside the rag she used to wash the dishes. After swiping her hands, she moved back to the table. "I ken everythin' is different from Skye. But I can promise ye this, Davina. If ye are a good person, truthful, and loyal, ye will be granted the same loyalty and love and will never again want for family."

Davina fidgeted at her words and then nodded.

"I ken life here will seem wild and strange for a while. But ye'll soon see how marvelous it is, Davina."

Slims stood in the barn and watched his boss and good friend, Frederick, walking toward him. Most of the chores were done, and Slims debated joining the men in the bunkhouse to play yet another game of poker. However, he yearned for the chance to set out on a long ride through the fields, returning at sunset. In the middle of winter, that wasn't possible.

He studied Frederick, sensing an undercurrent of frustration. He had seemed at ease with his wife at breakfast, and Slims wondered what had occurred after he left the kitchen. Slims leaned against one of the stalls, absently patting Boots's head, as he too watched Frederick approach. Boots was Frederick's prize chestnut filly with white around her ankles. She nickered, sticking out her nose, as though sniffing for a treat.

"Ah, girl, I forgot," Frederick soothed, as he ran a hand down her long jaw, giving it a good scratch. "Why can't all women be as uncomplicated as you?"

Slims stiffened as he focused on Frederick. At fifty-one, Slims was seventeen years older than Frederick, and he had watched the younger man grow up since he was a boy in the frontier town of Fort Benton. When Frederick's family had departed Fort Benton to find a homestead in Bear Grass Springs in 1864, Slims had joined them, as he already considered them his family. When Frederick's parents fought, and his mother abandoned them, Slims remained loyal to the boys, holding them as they cried, cleaning them up after they fought at school, and acting as an uncle to them. Even then, Frederick had been his favorite. Slims had liked Cole and Peter well enough, but Frederick had always treated Slims as family.

After a long moment of silence, Slims asked, "Was I wrong to bring her here, Boss?" Frederick stared at him long and hard. "Should I have brought her into town instead?"

Swearing under his breath, Frederick shook his head. "No. Then you'd have an irate Sorcha too. And that's the last thing we need in the middle of winter."

Chuckling, Slims shook his head. "None of us need that." Sobering, he focused on Frederick, who remained staring into space, as he absently patted his horse. "What bothers you, Boss?" Although they were friends and virtually family, Slims insisted on treating Frederick with respect. He wanted to set an example to all the men who worked on the ranch.

"I don't know what to make of Davina."

Slims stood silently waiting, knowing Frederick would eventually say more.

"She was shocked we would be on such friendly terms with our ranch hands. That you would be in the kitchen, having a meal with us." He stared at Slims and shook his head.

Slims stiffened, as though personally insulted. "She's the newcomer. She has no right to judge how we do things."

Nodding, Frederick sighed. "It makes no sense to me that she shows up in the middle of winter. What woman flees her home and arrives here in January?"

Slims stood in quiet contemplation. "I'm sorry, Boss. I shouldn't have taken her at her word and brought her here. I should have returned her to the station and told her to leave."

Frederick paced the barn. "No, that would have only stirred up a hornet's nest. You know Leena would have spoken to Annabelle, and then the MacKinnons would have wanted to hog-tie you for forcing a family member from town." He shared a rueful smile with Slims. "You know how they are about family."

"I don't want to let a viper into your home, Fred."

"She's no viper," he murmured, "but I don't know what she is." He shared a frustrated look with his foreman. "Come. Let's go check on Sugar. She'll need a little lovin'."

Slims chuckled, following Frederick to the stall of one of Frederick's pregnant mares. Three mares would foal this spring, and he suspected they'd have to build an addition onto the horse barn if Frederick didn't begin to sell his horses soon. However, Frederick hated the thought of selling any of the horses he'd raised, and Slims knew only time and patience would ease Frederick into the idea of parting with a beloved horse.

While Frederick looked over Sugar and reassured himself there were no imminent signs of her beginning the birthing process, Slims remained deep in thought. After Frederick joined him outside Sugar's stall, he asked, "Do you believe her story? That she came here to avoid an arranged marriage?"

"Aye," he said, "but I know there's more to it than that. She had already been married once, so why not accept it again? What would make a woman suddenly defiant?" Frederick shared a long look with his foreman. "I don't like the idea that trouble shadows her, Slims."

That afternoon, Davina reentered the kitchen when she heard the sound of many pans rattling. She paused at the incongruous sight of the giant of a man wearing an apron over his red flannel shirt and brown pants. Unable to fight off a giggle, she met his glower as he turned to the doorway.

"Thought you'd never show up," he muttered.

"You could have called for me," she snapped back, standing rigid, as though reprimanded by her overbearing da.

"No," Slims murmured, turning back to the countertop where he chopped a potato. "We know better than to make much noise." He pointed to the pans with his knife. "That was as much of a racket as I'd ever make."

He glanced at her over his shoulder and saw her staring at him in confusion. "The babes. None of us want to be responsible for waking them. For, if we are, Miss Sorcha's told us it's our responsibility to get them back to sleep." He smiled as she giggled. "And that is more than any of us could handle."

She sobered. "You don't like children."

His countenance softened, as though considering Sorcha's babies. "No, I adore those little ones. And I'd die protectin' them, if need be." He paused as though he were warning her of something, but, when she continued to stare at him in bewilderment, he returned his attention to the meal he was preparing. "I thought we'd make a stew for tonight."

"All ye need to do is teach me how to use this monstrosity, an' ye can return to the animals."

He made a disgusted noise and slammed the knife onto the chopping board. "I imagine a woman like you believes that's where a man like me belongs." He gazed at her with a knowing look, as she stared at him with dread. "A beast of a man belongs with the beasts, aye?" he said, mimicking her accent.

"I never said such a thing," she protested, flushing at his words.

"No, but I'm certain you thought it. And I know you were not pleased to have breakfast with the hands this morning." He faced her. "I'm sorry to disappoint you, miss, but life is hard on a ranch, and we'll grab at whatever joy we can find. That always includes a good meal and fine company. And, for your misfortune, your cousin is one of the finest women any of us has ever met."

When Davina stared at him as though he were a barbarian, he crossed his arms over his chest and smirked at her. "We know she's the boss's woman, and we'd never disrespect her," Slims said. "She treats all of us as though we are worthy of her regard and has never looked down at us, merely because we are hired hands." He waited, nodding his head, as she paled at the implication she had been rude and judgmental because she had done just that.

"Now I'm to teach you how to use this stove," he said, turning to it.

Although Slims spent many minutes describing how to use the beautiful stove, a stove Davina could only have dreamed about while in Scotland, her mind was muddled. At the end of his long tutorial, she remembered little of what he had said about how to regulate the heat in the main oven, how to use the warming oven, or how to heat water in the water vat. All she could see was the disapproval glinting in his gaze. All she could feel was the sinking sensation in her stomach that she had failed. Again.

Two days later, Slims entered the main house to help Davina cook supper. He hoped it was for the last time. Being close to her, but not truly forming a connection with her, was a torment. He knew she had no regard for him and resented the time he and the men spent in the main house. However, he dreaded the thaw worse, for that would mean drifters would arrive, looking for work. And, with the drifters, another cook was bound to appear. When that occurred, the men would take all their meals in the bunkhouse, and he would only ever see Davina in passing.

He waited in the kitchen for five long minutes, but, when she failed to appear, he swore. Rather than rattle pans and act like a demented fool, he walked on silent boot heels toward the hallway leading to a few family rooms on the main floor and the stairs to the second floor.

As he approached the hallway, two voices singing in perfect harmony floated down the hallway, and he paused. Never had he heard such beauty before. Although he had no idea what they were saying, the longing in their voices evoked a deep, unfulfilled yearning in him. For the love of a worthy woman. For a family of his own. To truly belong.

When the song ended, he let out a raspy breath, praying for another song to begin. When one did, he leaned against the wall, intent on not making any noise and unintentionally interrupting the impromptu serenade. This time the song was upbeat, almost cheerful, although the sense of pining for a lost love remained. When that song ended, he held his breath, letting it out with a disappointed huff when he heard voices chatting rather than another song starting.

He pushed away from the wall, moving toward the rear room where Sorcha spun her yarns. Inside the comfortable room, she had looms and mounds of wool to spin. An area in one corner had been barricaded off for the twins. They slept and played in it while their mother worked and seemed contented whenever they heard her voice and were near each other.

His breath caught as he saw Davina holding little Mairi, now one year old. Davina *coo*ed and whispered something in her cousin's ear, smiling as the girl tugged at her hair. The floorboard creaked, and she spun so Mairi was clasped to her front, protected from whoever intruded. At the sight of him, he saw her relax and then *coo* again at her cousin.

"Have you decided not to cook tonight, miss?" he asked.

Davina bounced Mairi in her arms and smiled at Slims. "Let's see if you can make him less of a grouch, aye?" she said. Handing Mairi to Slims, she raised an eyebrow in challenge, as though daring him to refuse to hold the beautiful baby.

He instinctively reached for her, cradling Mairi against his chest. "Hello, little love," he said, kissing her head. He swayed from side to side and chuckled when she grabbed his nose. Ignoring Davina and her shocked expression, he focused on Sorcha. "It's been too long since I've seen the babes. They're always asleep when we eat."

Sorcha smiled. "Aye, be thankful they are. They've taken to throwin' food. Yesterday we were covered in porridge when we were done feedin' the wee beasts." She held baby Harold high as she said that, laughing as he chortled.

Slims's attention was distracted when Mairi patted him on his cheeks and then rocked forward and back in his arms. "Oh, you think that's a fine adventure, don't you, Miss Mairi?" he murmured, kissing her on her forehead, as she collapsed forward onto his shoulder, heaving out a sigh and tumbling into sleep. "There's a little angel." He ran a big hand over her back, as he rocked from side to side.

When he caught Davina staring at him in abject wonder, he winked at her. "This isn't the first time I've held a baby, miss."

"Apparently not," she murmured. "How … fascinating." She flushed as he continued to stare at her. After a long moment, she cleared her throat and turned to Sorcha. "I believe I'm needed in the kitchen. Will ye be all right?"

Sorcha smiled. "Aye, Harold's about to fall asleep too." She motioned for Slims to follow her to the area in the corner of the room, where she laid Harold and then eased Mairi down. "They'll have their rest, an' then perhaps they'll join us at dinner tonight?"

Slims grimaced. "If we're to eat that supper, we had better start preparin' it." After following Davina out of the room, through the house, and into the kitchen, he paused. "What will you make tonight?"

She spun to stare at him in confusion. "I dinna understand," she whispered. "Why should it matter what I want to make?"

"Today's the last day I want to help you. I have important

work to do in the barns as we prepare for the upcoming season."

She turned away, her shoulders rigid as she yanked on an apron. "Important, aye. Of course."

Frowning, Slims studied her. "I'm hired here on the ranch as foreman. To oversee the workings of the ranch and the men. Not to cook. You do understand the distinction, miss?"

She flushed and bowed her head.

He tilted her chin up with the subtle strength of two fingers under her chin. "But that doesn't mean that what you do isn't as important. Or that I'm not grateful for the delicious meals you cook." He waited for her to meet his implacable stare, confusion and concern shining in his gaze as he saw the defeat in hers. "Davina, what did I do?"

"Nothin'," she whispered, her mouth clamped shut after the single word escaped. "Nothin'."

Slims's gaze focused even more on her, and his hold on her altered as his hand cupped her cheek. "When a woman says *nothing*, I know I messed up. When she says it more than once, I know I hurt her." He waited, as though hoping she would make some response. When she remained resolutely silent, he stroked a thumb over the soft skin of her cheek, seemingly fascinated as a faint blush bloomed in the wake of his caress. "What did I do?"

She shook her head and took a step back, effectively separating from him. "Ye showed me where I stand. And, for that, I'm most grateful." She turned away, her shoulders rising and falling, as she took labored breaths. "I believe I do not need yer help, Mr. Slims. Ye've been most kind takin' time from yer busy day to show me how to use the stove. I ken I'll be fine."

"Miss," Slims said in a deep melodious voice. He noted she shivered at his voice but did not turn to face him.

"No, sir. I thank ye." She looked over one shoulder, her

expression carefully blank and free of all emotion. "Ye should return to yer *important* work." Nodding to the kitchen door, she waited expectantly for him to leave.

With one last tormented stare, Slims swore under his breath and marched out the door, slamming it shut behind him. When he stood outside, he waited a few minutes on the steps, hoping the cold and the slight wind would cool his irrational anger. However, he could not determine if he was angry with himself or her.

CHAPTER 3

A few days later, Davina wandered out of the main house from the kitchen door. For the past few days, the weather had reminded her of Scotland. Gray and gloomy, although there hadn't been much snow. The previous evening at supper, Dalton and Dixon had entertained her with tales about the harsh winter of 1886–87, where every day felt like a blizzard, and they lost upward of 60 percent of their cattle. And those cattle that had survived were emaciated to the point of falling over with a strong gust of wind.

Shorty only chimed in to regale her about the day he rode in with a herd of healthy cattle, after wintering in the high country meadow, surviving on rationed tins of beans in a rickety cabin. He had puffed out his chest with pride that he had helped save the ranch from foreclosure.

"Miraculous," she whispered to herself, envisioning the scene. She couldn't imagine what Frederick, who had worked his entire adult life to ensure the ranch's success, had felt. It must have been like waking from the worst nightmare and having every dream answered. "I wonder what that feels like."

She gave a small shake of her head and stared at the snow-covered land. She knew the mountains were in the distance, but low-lying clouds shrouded them today. Turning her focus to the ranch, her glance roved over the barns, the paddocks, the chicken coop, and the small smithy. Everything needed to keep the ranch self-sufficient and running smoothly. After all of Frederick's hard work, she couldn't imagine losing the ranch due to the fickleness of the weather.

Wandering in the direction of the larger of the two barns, she ignored the rope tied between it and the main house—there in case of a blizzard—walking freely to the barn door and easing it open. Once inside, she waited a few moments for her eyes to adjust and then sighed with pleasure. She'd always loved horses, although her da had informed her that horses were a man's domain.

When a horse poked its head over the stall door and nickered, as though it wanted attention, she moved to it. Stroking a hand down its nose, she giggled as it snuffled. "I have no treat for ye," she whispered. "Although I'd love to take ye out on a ride, ye beautiful beast."

"That's Frederick's prize filly. He wouldn't be pleased to know you'd stolen her," Slims said, smiling as she gasped and spun to face him. "She's Boots." He chuckled when Boots poked her head out again, nudging at Davina's shoulder for more attention.

Davina patted at Boots, scratching behind her ears. "*Boots.* What an odd name for such a beautiful lady."

"She has white markings from hoof to knee on all four limbs," Slims said with a wave in the direction of her hooves. "You seem fond of horses."

"Aye," she said, as she smiled and patted again at Boots. "I've always loved them. But I ken I'm foolish."

"Why?" he asked with a quizzical frown. "Do you feel that way, or did someone make you feel that way?"

Davina flushed and shrugged, ignoring his question. She dropped her hand from Boots's muzzle and backed up a step, facing Slims.

After a moment, Slims looked at her in confusion. "Why are you here? Do you need help in the kitchen?"

Davina stomped her foot on the ground and let out a huff of frustration. "As though the only reason I'd venture into the barn is because I'd be lookin' for yer help," she muttered.

He closed the distance between them, his gaze filled with annoyance. "No, miss. I know I'm the last person you'd ever seek out for any aid. Why would you look to a dirty cowpoke for that?" When she stared at him in befuddlement, he nodded. "Aye, I can only imagine your continued disgust at having to mingle with the hands at meals. Why bother feignin' interest when Dix tells his stories?"

She let out a raspy breath and shook her head. "'Tisn't a pretense. I like hearin' what life on the ranch is like. An' I can only imagine the amount of hard work ye do every day to ensure it keeps runnin'."

Shaking his head, Slims continued to stare at her, as though she were a magician, intent on tricking him. "I know you don't like us mingling with you at meals, Davina. I know you wish we were in the bunkhouse."

She faced him, her neck arched back so she could look up into his eyes as he loomed over her. "Ye dinna ken anythin'. Seein' ye, watchin' ye interact every day with yer men …" Her voice broke off, as a fine quiver ran through her.

"What?" he rasped, his hand rising to brush Boots away from nudging her shoulder again. Inadvertently he stroked her cheek.

"How can I no' admire a man who leads by example? Who could bellow and badger those around him to do what he wants, but he doesna." She dropped her gaze, flushing, as

41

though she had said more than she wanted and wished she could call back her words.

"You barely spare me a glance," he whispered in a near growl.

Her head jerked up, and she met his inquisitive gaze, his brown eyes glowing with a fierce emotion. "I dinna need to." She leaned forward, sniffing the air. "Yer footsteps and yer scent herald yer arrival." She closed her eyes a moment, as though savoring the scent of him, a woodsy, musky scent, mixed with horses and sweat. "Ye sit in the same spot every day. An', when ye speak, everyone listens."

"Miss," he breathed.

"I always ken when ye are near." She bit her lip, flushing again, and took a step away from him. She stilled her movements when he reached forward, softly gripping her arm. With a defiant tilt of her chin, she said, "Besides, ye never acknowledge me."

With a groan, he hauled her close, wrapping his strong arms tenderly around her. One arm banded around her back, the other held her head as he lowered his mouth, capturing her gasp with a deeply drugging kiss. He slanted his mouth over hers, kissing her with passionate desperation. As though frustrated with their height difference, he hefted her up and set her on a pile of hay, bringing her closer to shoulder level. Her hands fluttered around his shoulders, as soft and as fleeting as the caress of a butterfly's wings, and he yearned for more of her touch.

She matched him, kiss for kiss, as wild for him as he was for her. Her hands rose, tracing through his hair, before linking behind his neck and holding him close, as though she were afraid he'd disappear. When he lifted his head, peppering kisses down her cheek and neck, "Nae," she gasped. "Dinna stop."

His breaths heated her skin, as he buried his face in her

neck. "I have to, miss. Or I fear I won't be able to. And then you'll have no choice."

At his words, she stiffened and pushed at him. "Nae," she moaned. "Nae," she said, as she pushed harder, nearly tumbling off the hay in her urgency to be free of his touch.

He glared at her, as his breath continued to saw in and out of him. However, after ensuring she would not fall, he kept his hands fisted at his side. "You wanted me to kiss you as much as I wanted to kiss you."

At his proclamation, she muttered, "Ye dinna have to make me sound like a harlot!" When she dared to meet his gaze and saw amusement mixed with concern, the rosy blush brought on by their bout of passion faded, and she stared at him with wide-eyed horror. "What must ye think of me?" She raised a shaking hand to her head, as her eyes widened with shame. "I'm no' a loose woman, Slims. No matter how I acted today. I swear to you, I—"

He made a hushing noise. "Of course you aren't. If you were, you would have taken up the invitation the others had quietly given you." When she frowned at him, he sighed and rubbed at his head. "You never understood that Dixon and Dalton were seein' if you were free for courtin'?"

"Courtin'?" she gasped, as though the entire notion were preposterous. "Why would they want to court me?"

He shook his head. "If you're unable or unwillin' to see why, I'm not the one to explain it to you." He let out a deep sigh. "I apologize if I offended you, miss. I never meant to." He closed his eyes, as though experiencing severe pain. "I … Forgive me." After one last searing look, he spun on his heels and stormed away.

Davina waited, until she heard the barn door slam, before she crumpled to her knees, her legs shaking so hard that she knew she wouldn't make it a step without collapsing. *What must he think of me?* she asked herself over and over. She refused to answer the question of why the answer mattered to her so very much.

~

Slims stormed from the barn, blind to where he was going. His only goal to put as much distance between him and that infuriating woman. He sighed when he had marched into the far reaches of the paddock and slung his arms over the railing. Ignoring the freezing temperature and the scent of snow in the air, he forced himself to calm. To ignore the overwhelming desire to return to the barn, find an empty stall, and love her until neither of them knew their names.

He let out a shaky breath and then another, as he prayed for the cold to put a damper on his ardor. Nothing could have prepared him for her soft admission. For her confession that she was as attuned to him as he was to her. Not a day passed that he didn't long to see her. No matter that he had attempted to ignore her. It had all been in vain.

Clinging to Frederick's words, Slims had fed his anger that she hadn't wanted the hands to eat with them. Even as each meal, where she had shown a warm welcome and a genuine interest in all present, had proven there had been a misunderstanding, Slims had chosen to nurture his resentment. Anything to protect himself from the growing attraction he had for her.

"Look how well that worked," he muttered, hitting his fist on the railing, as his mind filled with the sensation and the memory of holding her. Kissing her. Feeling her desire match his. Never had he thought to know such passion from a mere kiss. He rubbed at his lips, feeling bereft that they were parted from hers.

"Fool," he admonished himself. With a long sigh, he knew

he must avoid being alone with her again. She was a drug he could not become addicted to, for she could never be his.

A week later toward the end of January, Slims sat at the kitchen table, sipping at his coffee, after eating his fill of the simple, delicious breakfast Davina had prepared for them. He hid his smile behind his coffee cup as he watched her battle embarrassment as Dixon flirted with her. He wasn't overly concerned, as she seemed more flustered than charmed by the younger man's attentions. She had grown increasingly disconcerted during the past week, now that she knew the man wasn't just chattering at her but flirting with her.

Slims raised an eyebrow as Frederick entered the kitchen and smiled at everyone, although Frederick's hair stuck out at odd angles, and he had dark circles under his eyes. Battling a yawn, Frederick sat in his customary chair. "I trust everyone had a restful evening." He grimaced as he looked at Davina. "Well, except for you, cousin. I fear you suffered as Sorcha and I did."

"What happened, Boss?" Dalton asked, as he sipped at his coffee. He eyed the platter of bacon, as though deciding if he wanted another serving.

"The babes are teething, and they weren't shy about hiding their misery last night." He yawned hugely, stretching his arms overhead. "Sorcha's abed. Mairi and Harold are finally asleep and will hopefully rest for another hour or so."

The men nodded and began to speak in barely audible whispers. "Will they be all right, Boss?" Dixon asked. He jumped as Shorty belted him on his arm and shook his head at him. "Well, it's a decent question."

"They're teething, boy. Every baby has to get his teeth. I'm sure you drove your mama mad when you got yours."

Dixon shrugged, as the other men snickered.

Frederick moved to pour himself a cup of coffee and gazed outside. "Looks like as fine a day as we'll have for a while." He glanced over his shoulder at Slims. "Do you think you could make it to town?"

Slims rose and looked out the window. "If I go alone, there will be little to worry about."

Shaking his head, Frederick slurped a sip of the hot drink. "No, you know Davina has to go with you. To attempt to retrieve her trunk." He looked out at the cloud-covered sky. "What do you think?"

Slims swore under his breath. "Damned if I know. It's been like this for over a week and barely snowed enough to cover a hoof print." He leaned his hip against the counter. "It's still, but that could be a sign of calm weather or a wicked storm brewin'."

Frederick nodded. "I agree. It's your decision. But, if you're going, go soon." He slapped his friend on his shoulder, before returning to the table and smiling at Davina, who had watched their interaction with concern in her gaze.

Slims quietly shut the kitchen door behind him and strode outside to stand near the drive, as he looked to the heavens and breathed deeply of the clear, cold air. At times he thought he could smell snow on the breeze, but today all he noted was an increased chill. He had read about the use of barometers to aid in predicting weather changes, but they did not have such a device at the ranch. Instead he had to try to read the weather, which was an imprecise art.

Shorty sidled up next to him. "What do you think?"

Slims stared at the overcast sky. "I think everything would be simpler if I could hightail into and out of town by myself. But Boss wants me to take her. And that makes everything more complicated." He shook his head in dismay. "What do you think, Short?"

"We haven't had snow for days. It doesn't feel any different today than it has since the last big snow two weeks ago. There's no reason the weather won't hold long enough for you to race in and out of town. As long as that woman doesn't have a mind to shop at the store."

Slims chuckled. "She doesn't strike me as a woman with a hankerin' for fine china and lace. But what do I know?" He shared an amused glance with his friend. "I'll inform Boss, and then I'll help you ready the sleigh and horses."

Shorty nodded, walking toward the barn.

Slims took one last glance at the sky, fighting a sinking sensation that, no matter what he did, it would be the wrong decision. "Well, might as well do somethin'," he muttered, as he moved to the house to inform Davina to prepare for their quick trip into town.

After snuggling under the blankets beside Slims, Davina worried that a residual awkwardness would exist between them after their kiss a week ago. However, Slims stared at the horses and the snow covered road and acted as though she weren't even present. Although she knew she should be offended, a wave of exhaustion engulfed her. She yawned and valiantly fought to remain awake.

However, after her near-sleepless night with the twins crying their agony over their teething, she lost her battle, and her head bobbed with the sleigh's movements. Soon it came to rest on Slims's shoulder, where she unconsciously curled farther into his warmth.

Slims swore, and the sleigh veered off the road. Davina jerked awake. Screeching, she gripped the edge of the seat and the sleigh, fighting being thrown from it, as the sleigh rocked precariously before coming to a precipitous halt. She peered over the blanket, where a fierce gust of wind froze her exposed skin and made her even more reluctant to leave her warm cocoon. Instead, she scooted over to nestle against the large man. "Why is it already night?" she asked around a huge yawn, intent on resuming her nap.

"It's not," he half yelled to be heard over the wind as he gasped for breath. "A storm hit, and we were halfway between town and the ranch. I had hoped we could make it to Leena and Karl's, but I can't see anything."

She sat up, the blanket dropping around her waist, and she belatedly realized it was covered in inches of snow. "We canna stay here overnight." Davina stared at Slims with dawning horror, as she began to comprehend the gravity of their predicament.

Slims shook his head. "No. And pray this storm blows out tonight. We wouldn't want to be stranded here for days." With those ominous words, he tied down the reins and hopped from the sleigh. After patting each horse on the head, he walked away, disappearing after a few steps into the storm.

"Ye canna think to leave me here!" Davina cried out. "I ken I'm not the ideal woman, but ye canna be that cruel." She stared out into the overwhelming gray and whiteness as snow continued to fall. Fighting an almost uncontrollable panic, she forced herself to remain seated in the sleigh, tugging the blanket around her shoulders. Rather than praying for the storm to end quickly, her prayers were simpler. Over and over, she repeated in her mind, *Please come back. Please come back*, as tears silently coursed down her cheeks. A wicked wind began to howl, freezing her tears on her cheeks, and she tugged the blanket over her again, any perception of safety and comfort vanquished by a sense of impending doom.

"Miss?"

She leaned forward at the faint call.

"Slims?" she screamed. "Slims!"

"Keep callin' my name. I can't make heads nor tails of where I am."

Davina continued to call out to him, her prayer for him to return to her answered when he suddenly appeared beside her. She jumped at his sudden reappearance. "Slims," she gasped.

"Thank God, woman," he murmured. He shivered as another cold breeze blew. "If we're fortunate, I'll be able to walk the horses and the sleigh to a nearby cabin." He extracted a rope from the back of the sleigh and moved to the front of the team, where he tied it to the harness between the two horses. It was a novice way of moving the team, but he kept a short lead on the animals and soothed them with his soft voice, as they walked gingerly forward.

Davina sat in the sleigh, huddled under her blanket, clinging to hope that they would arrive to the cabin safely. They moved in jerky motions but always in a forward manner. After what seemed like an eternity, but what she knew was most likely only a matter of less than one-quarter of an hour, she faintly heard Slims say, "Whoa," to the horses. "Are we there?" she called out, to be heard over the wind.

"Yes," he yelled. "Wait for me." He appeared and held out his arms. "Let me carry you." Without waiting for her response, he picked her up and slung her into his arms. "You'd have fallen in the deep snow." He trudged with steady strides through the ever-deepening snow toward a dark mass which took shape as a cabin only as they were upon it. Shielding her with his body, he flung the door open and set her inside. "I'll be back after I've tended the horses. Try to stay warm."

She gaped after him as the door slammed shut. After a moment filled with shock and uncertainty, she shook the snow-covered blanket out near the door and fought bone-deep shivers. Long shadows filled the single room, with the frigid air seeping in through gaps in the wood planks and under the door. A pallet of sorts was in one corner, but there was no stove or anything else that would warm them.

She moved away from the door, toward the pallet, pulling her coat tightly around her. After she sat on the pallet, she wrapped the blanket around her, trying to envision a warm day in the Highlands. The feel of the sun on her face. Anything to banish the sense of dread and doom as the gusts rattled the small cabin, making it feel as though it were to be torn to pieces at any moment.

She stared at the door, willing Slims to return. She instinctively knew that, if he failed to return, she would not survive this ordeal. His presence was intrinsically tied to her enduring this nightmare experience. After what seemed like an eternity, and, as the storm raged and as the sky darkened even further, the door rattled open. At first, she feared the wind had burst it open, and she gave a small scream in fright. But then she recognized Slims standing there, shaking and quivering.

Pushing herself up, she tripped on the blanket and raced to him. "Come away from the door, Slims," she said, tugging on his arm. "Come inside."

"It's barely warmer in here than out there," he muttered, dropping the objects in his arms.

She looked down, seeing the fur blanket that lined the sleigh and another blanket. "Come to the pallet." She urged him to sit down, but, as her hands roved over him, while flinging the blanket around his shoulders, she realized he was soaked through. "Take your clothes off." She flushed at the command but then ignored any sense of wickedness or shamelessness as he shook in her arms.

"I can't make my fingers work the buttons," he stammered out.

With a disgruntled mutter, Davina moved in front of him, her fingers agile and born of desperation, as she freed him of first his coat and then of his waistcoat and shirt. "Why ye chose today of all days to wear so many clothes," she muttered.

"I was goin' to town," he shivered out. "Like to look my best as the foreman."

She bit her lip at any further complaints, her hands pausing at his pants. She shared a long look with him and then worked on those fastenings too.

"I'll leave my underthings on," he said.

"Ye willna," she snapped. "I was a married woman. Ye willna shock me into a faint." She motioned for him to strip as she moved away to gather blankets to wrap around him. When she saw white underclothes join the pile of his clothes, she handed him a blanket, waiting a few moments before turning to fuss over him. "We'll wrap this one around ye to get ye nice an' warm."

"Nothin' but your body heat will work," Slims said, as he groaned, falling backward onto the pallet. "God, just let me sleep."

"Nae!" Davina cried, pouncing on him. "Ye are no' to sleep. Do ye hear me?"

"The dead could hear your screeching," he muttered. He batted at her hands. "Quit pokin' at me, woman."

"I'm pokin' at ye so ye'll sit up. Ye need to stay awake. Ye canna sleep, Slims. If ye do, ye may never wake again."

He let out a deep breath. "Perhaps that wouldn't be such a bad thing," he muttered.

"Nae," Davina cried again. "Nae, ye willna die. Ye canna, ye daft man."

Opening one eye, he stared at her, as a smile played around his lips. "For a small woman, you are very bossy." He stared at her a long moment and then smiled fully.

"An' why should that amuse ye?" Davina asked, as she snuggled up against him, ignoring his grunts and groans of protest. When she was comfortable, she pulled the last blanket over them, covering them both.

"I'm not amused," he said, as he wrapped an arm around her waist. "I feel like a fool, for I should never have doubted you were Sorcha's cousin." He made a soothing sound, as she stiffened in his hold. "If I'd seen you acting like this at the ranch, I would never have worried."

Davina rested for a long moment with her back to his front, her fingers absently playing with the hairs on his forearm. "Ye worried about me?"

"I sure as hell did," Slims slurred, grunting when she elbowed him in his belly to wake up. "Frederick and Miss Sorcha are the closest I have to family. As I'll ever have."

She pressed closer to him as a bout of shivering overcame him. She ran her feet up and down his legs, quivering with the cold that emanated from him. "I thought most men were furnaces," she muttered.

He chuckled. "We are when we haven't spent too long in a blizzard."

She yelped when she inadvertently touched his freezing feet. "Oh, yer puir wee feet!" she gasped. "We must warm them." She ignored him and wriggled around until his feet were wrapped up more securely in the outermost blanket. She soon realized that would be insufficient to warm them. "We should wrap the fur around yer feet for a while."

"Can't you stay still for one minute?" Slims complained, as she elbowed him in his chest and crawled over him, rearranging blankets as she tugged the fur to his feet. She wrapped up his feet, holding the fur over his frozen feet and pressing the wrapped bundle to her chest. He stared at her in wonder, whispering, "Heaven."

"What?" she asked, her brown eyes lit with purpose and determination.

"I've died, and I'm in heaven," he said a moment before he passed out.

Davina gaped at him, wondering if the wind had played tricks with her hearing. Rather than beat on his leg to wake him up, she watched the steady rise and fall of his chest to reassure herself that he slept due to exhaustion, not due to a near-death experience. Although she was chilled, helping Slims had aided in calming her fears.

She waited a quarter hour, felt his feet again, and sighed with relief to find they were not nearly as cold. After rewrapping them, she crawled up his body, nestling against him once more as she tucked the blankets around them. With a sigh of contentment, she relaxed further as Slims wrapped an arm around her belly, pulling her close.

"Sleep, love," he murmured in her ear.

She smiled, for once following his command without qualm.

An eerie silence woke him. Slims's head jerked up, as though a clap of thunder had sounded. Cocking his head to one side, no sound could be heard. The ferocious winds from the night before had completely calmed, and now the silence was nearly deafening. He blearily stared around the room, his gaze taking in the scattered mass of his clothes tossed in a haphazard mess on the floor. Belatedly he realized he held a warm

53

woman in his arms, and he stilled his motions, eager not to wake her.

He gazed down at the woman cradled in his arms, marveling that she was here. The last thing he remembered from the previous day was her warming his feet by holding them pressed against her chest. With a groan, he dropped his head back, fighting the image of her caring for him in such a tender way. No one had shown him such regard since he was a young man. Since he had learned the meaning of betrayal. He fought against softening any more toward her, but he knew it was futile. Her actions from the previous day had earned her his loyalty.

She murmured and stirred, rubbing her face against the blanket resting on his chest. He felt an irrational jealousy for the blanket feeling the softness of her skin, rather than him. He raised one of his large hands to smooth away strands of her hair that had fallen into her eyes.

"*Shh*, darlin', you're well," he murmured.

She sat up with a start, elbowing him in his belly.

"*Oof*," he muttered. "I remember that well." He watched her with an amused glint in his eyes, the laugh lines around his eyes crinkling as he fought a smile. "Remind me not to anger you in the future."

"What am I doin' here in yer arms?" she gasped, wriggling against him.

"Hold still, or you will soon have an emergency," he muttered. When she froze, he chuckled. "I thought you said that you'd been married and that you weren't easily shocked."

"I lied!" she gasped, as her bare foot ran up and down his calf, earning a groan from him.

"You were never married?" he asked, as he took deep breaths in and out in an attempt to calm his reaction to her.

"Nae, I'm easily shocked."

He sputtered out a laugh and fell to his back, tumbling

her with him. She shrieked but grabbed onto his strong arm and settled to his side. The blankets continued to cover them, although the one she had used to cover his nakedness was in danger of sliding free. "Oh, miss, you are a treasure."

She froze at his words. "I ken what I am, and I am no treasure." She wriggled in his arms in an attempt to free herself from his hold, finally giving up with a huff when he kept one strong arm around her. "I'd think ye'd ken when a woman doesna want yer attentions."

Tracing a finger over her flushed cheek, he smiled. His eyes were filled with delight as he stared at her flushed face, relaxed after sleeping in his arms all night. She had creases on her cheek and forehead from the blanket, and he held himself back from leaning forward to kiss along the irregular line. "You're beautiful, miss. Any man who doesn't see that is a fool." He frowned as he felt her stiffen again at his compliment. "Why do you discredit any praise?"

She buried her face in the blanket, hiding her expression from him.

"What was your husband like?" Slims asked in a gentle voice.

Her head jerked up, and she gaped at him in astonishment. "Why would ye ask about the man when I'm lyin' in yer arms, an' ye're as naked as the day ye were born?"

He chuckled and shook his head with remorse. "If we'd done something more than share our combined body heat so we wouldn't freeze to death, I'd refrain from asking about the man, for I'd hope your thoughts would only be about me." He gazed deeply into her eyes. "If this meant more than an act of mercy on your part, I'd roll you under me and act as though the blizzard still raged. Act like we had a stove and food and water, where we could remain here for days." His thumb traced her lower lip, his breath catching as she nibbled at it.

"Slims," she breathed, as she wiggled around so they rested chest to chest.

"Simon," he whispered. "My name is Simon." He ducked his head like a young boy, afraid of what the woman he adored most in the world would say.

A bright smile burst forth, and she cupped his face with both of her hands. "*Simon*," she murmured, her fingers delicately stroking through his hair. "A perfect name for ye."

"No one's called me that since I was a lad." His eyes shone with vulnerability and trepidation. His gaze seared her with its intensity. "Trust me."

"I'm layin' with ye, and yer clothes are across the room," she teased. "I must trust ye." She bit her lip and sobered. "My husband was no' a nice man. He tried, ye ken?" she said in a rush of words, as she saw Slims fighting indignation at the implication she had been harmed. "He never raised a hand against me, aye?"

Slims caressed her shoulder and then ran his fingers through her silky hair that had come loose from its knot tied at her nape. It looked like a shaft of sunlight spread out on the pillow and blanket.

In an almost dreamy voice, lost to her memories, she said, "But he never understood me, and he did no' care to. He wanted a dutiful wife. A wife who did no' think, who did no' dream. An' he wanted bairns." She shrugged. "An' we had bairns."

At the whispered agony in her voice at the last sentence, Slims's caress gentled even further, and he made a murmur of distress on her part.

"We had three bairns together, but none lived longer than six months," she said, as a few tears coursed down her cheeks. "I miss them every day."

He pulled her closer, urging her head to his chest as his

arms banded around her. "Of course you do," he murmured. "What did your husband do?"

She let out a huff of breath, pushing herself up. "There's really no more to say, Slims." She spun away so quickly from him, flushing furiously when she saw him resting with a blanket only covering him like a loin cloth, that she toppled off their pallet to the floor.

Watching her with a wary expression as she became pricklier, while patting down her rumpled clothes and ratted hair, he nodded. "Oh, I think there's plenty more to be said, miss. But I should dress. And we should go to town. And then we'll see what shouldn't be done."

CHAPTER 4

Slims shivered in the sleigh as they made slow progress into town. Although he'd had to wade through nearly waist-high drifts to make a path for the sleigh and the horses to reach the road, once they had attained the roadway, Slims found marks, signaling another had already ventured to or from town. His clothes had barely dried from the night before, and the warmth he had felt upon wakening seemed a distant memory. A precious memory.

Casting a furtive glance at his passenger in the sleigh, Davina sat hunched on the far side of the sleigh, seated as far away from him as possible. She glanced at the sea of sparkling white snow as though she had never seen such a majestic sight before. However, Slims knew from Sorcha that it snowed in Scotland, so he knew that Davina had seen fresh snow before.

"Davina, I know you loathe me, but I'm freezin'. Will you please sit closer to me?" When she threw an incredulous glare at him over her shoulder and tossed her head back in a defiant nature, he let out a huff. "That's it." Holding the reins with one hand, he reached for her, tugging her toward him.

He ignored her indignant shriek, tucking her into his side. "I'm not corrupting you," he snapped, as she batted at him. "I'm cold, and I can see you shivering over there too. We have to share body heat on a day like today. Stop being petulant."

At his words, she froze and became docile, as she sat with stooped shoulders beside him.

"What's come over you?" he asked, as he took the reins by both hands again.

"Nothin'," she said, pulling the blanket around him and then herself. "You're right. I was selfish, sitting separate in the corner."

He sat in quiet contemplation, as the harness jangled and the sound of the horse's hooves made soft *clop* noises on the fresh snow. Suddenly he wanted to learn anything and everything about her; yet he refrained from asking any intrusive questions. He had to bite his tongue to prevent a deluge of queries from bursting forth. He knew her first husband had damaged her spirit, and he vowed he would only bring her joy. With a sigh, he focused on the scenery.

A piercingly beautiful blue sky overhead, with clouds in the distance promising the potential for more snow, made the day seem even brighter after the dreariness of the previous days. A quick glance at the sun and Slims knew it had to be near to midday. "I doubt we'll have time to gather what we need and return to the ranch today. It's already too late in the day."

"It canna be," she murmured.

He shrugged. "There's not much daylight this time of year, and it took longer than I would have liked to hitch up the team and to clear a path to the road." He rubbed at his stomach that growled its hunger. "There's a hotel in town, miss."

She nodded, slinking farther down as she tugged the blanket to her chin.

He glowered at the blanket, wishing he could rip it off her, as he felt she used it as a shield to separate herself from him. However, he'd never intentionally harm her, and it was too cold to be without proper cover. "And you have family in town."

After a long moment, when he feared he would be consigned to carrying on a one-sided conversation, she said, "I doubt they will be as welcoming, warm, or trusting as Sorcha."

He laughed. "I think you will be surprised."

The sleigh curved around a bend, and they came upon Leena's house. He slowed the sleigh when the front door opened. Rather than Leena, a large man exited. "Karl!" Slims called out. "How did you fare with the blizzard?"

"Oh, we were fine, *ja*," he said with a smile. "Had a fire with my Leena and my Mette in my arms." His curious gaze roved from Slims to the woman cuddled beside him.

Slims nodded and smiled. "I'm escorting Miss Sorcha's cousin to town to retrieve her trunk and to get supplies for the ranch. I'm glad you're well. Say hello to Leena for us." He raised a hand.

"Another storm's coming!" Karl called out, as the sleigh began to move.

"Thank you!" Slims said, waving, as they moved away from Karl's house and toward town.

Davina looked at him in confusion. "Why don't you like him? He seemed nice, and Leena treated me well."

"Of course I like him," he said, "but we need to get to town."

After a few more minutes, they approached the outskirts of the town of Bear Grass Springs. On the right was the school and church, while, on the left, a blacksmith shop was near a large livery. "That livery is owned by your cousins," he said. He didn't slow their progress through town as they sped past a general store, a café, a bakery, a newspaper office, and a bank. There were saloons too, although she didn't focus on the names. She only looked to the buildings on the right side of the street as they drove through town, determined to do the same as they departed.

"That bakery we passed is also owned by your cousin, as is the newspaper shop," Slims said. "And the café is run by Frederick's grandparents."

"My family is that important in this town?" she whispered.

He chuckled. "Yes. When they speak, others listen." He shrugged. "There are always those who are jealous of their influence, but then they are generally not worth worryin' about."

She nodded and took a deep breath as they arrived at the small train station.

After tying up the reins, Slims held out his arm for her to help her from the sleigh. He sent her a fierce look when she paused in placing her hand on his arm, frowning when he felt her fingers trembling on his jacket. "All will be well, miss."

"Davina," she whispered. "Please call me Davina. *Miss* is too impersonal."

He paused, partway up the train station steps, his gaze locked with hers. "Davina," he said with a smile. "Come." He led her inside the small waiting room and called out to the stationmaster.

"Hello, sir," Davina said, "I've returned to collect my trunk."

The stationmaster blanched. "But it was already collected for you. Days ago."

"By whom?" Davina demanded. "Who would steal my things?"

"*Shh*, miss," Slims said in a warning voice. "Did one of the MacKinnons come by?"

"Yes, Mr. Slims. That young whippersnapper Ewan was here. Charming as always, although you'll know he's a father now."

Slims schooled his features into one of mild interest. "Yes, how wonderful for him. If you'll excuse us, we'll seek him out." Slims pushed Davina toward the exit. "Hush," he muttered, when she began to protest. "All is well. Ewan is Sorcha's brother. Although I don't know how he's a father. Jessamine wasn't with babe the last I saw her." He frowned and shook his head in confusion. Motioning for Davina to hop back in the sleigh, he followed her in.

"We'll stop at the store first, so Tobias can fill our order and then seek out the MacKinnons. I have a feeling you'll have a long visit with them."

~

Davina wandered outside the larger of the two stores in the town of Bear Grass Springs, the one Slims called the Merc, as he spoke to the proprietor, Tobias Sutton. She had learned that Tobias was also related to Frederick, although she wasn't certain how they were related. It seemed that everyone in this town was related to her family in one way or another. She glanced across the road, looking past the hotel and a lawyer's office, to watch with curiosity as men entered and exited a saloon called the Stumble-Out. A few seemed unsteady on their feet, and she grinned that the establishment had been aptly named.

When a few of the saloon patrons watched her with unveiled interest, she turned her focus to the impressive two-story hotel. Although she relished the thought of a warm bath, she did not have any coin to pay for a stay there, and she dreaded being in Sorcha's debt any more than she already was. She spun around at the sound of a grating voice.

"What do we have here?" a woman asked in a harsh, critical rasp. "I had thought you would know to go to the Boudoir. They are always looking for fresh blood."

"Boudoir?" Davina asked with a crinkle in her brows. "I dinna ken what ye mean." The older woman gripped Davina's wrist, and she gasped in pain at the tight clasp.

"Don't tell me that you're one of them." The woman's eyes shone with a mixture of glee and torment as she beheld Davina. The older woman stood ramrod straight and was so thin that it appeared the strong winds from yesterday could have blown her to the next Territory. Frayed around the edges, her black coat showed its age and hinted at her poverty.

"One of whom, ma'am?" Davina asked, tugging on her arm to free herself, but unable to.

"A MacKinnon," the woman hissed. "A murderer."

"Nae, I'm nae MacKinnon," Davina said with a cunning smile, "although I hope to ken them. I've heard they are an honorable, loyal family."

The woman made a sound akin to a growl as her hold on Davina tightened. "They wouldn't know the meaning of the word *honorable* if it bit them on their behind." She took in a deep stuttering breath. "If there was any justice in this world, they'd be in jail for the murder of my son."

Davina schooled her expression into one of mild interest. "I'm certain ye are mistaken."

The crone raised a gnarled finger and rasped, "They harbored a brutal horse in their livery and rejoiced when my Walter was trampled to death. If the lawyer wasn't in cahoots with them, I would have had justice!"

Davina stared at her with compassion but remained quiet.

The older woman huffed out an aggrieved breath, and her astute gaze roved over Davina, as she tilted her head to one side. "You're rather disheveled, dear."

Davina bristled. "'Tis what happens when ye're stranded in the middle of a blizzard," she snapped. She bit her lip as though instantly understanding she had said too much. At that moment, Slims emerged from the store, the door's bell jingling a warning as to his arrival. The older woman released Davina's arm and took a step back.

"Mrs. Jameson," Slims said with the merest of nods. "Always … interestin' to see you."

"It's a pleasure, you giant oaf," she snapped. Her gaze traveled from Slims to Davina and back again. "You came into town together. I'd know if you'd been here any amount of time. Men in this town are fools for new women."

Davina stiffened but said nothing more, while Slims stared at Mrs. Jameson with a bored expression.

"I wonder what the townsfolk will make of the news I have to impart?" she asked with a gleeful chortle. She pushed past them to walk down the boardwalk.

Davina watched her and shook her head in confusion. "What was that about?" she asked.

In a low voice, Slims asked, "What did you say to her?"

Davina closed her eyes and whispered, "She criticized my clothes. Said I belonged in a place called the Boudoir. And I snapped at her that I'd been stranded in a blizzard."

Slims's eyes widened, and he stared down the boardwalk to follow the back of the town's busybody. "Oh no," he breathed. "She'll turn last night's desire not to freeze into a night of lustful lovemaking."

Davina blushed. "Nae need to sound so horrified," she snapped, as she moved to walk around Slims, although she had no idea where she was to go. She just felt a need to move.

Slims gripped her arm, holding it gently, but preventing

her from moving away. "Don't you understand what she'll do? She'll ruin you, Davina. She'll turn your life into a living hell."

She shook her head. "I ken what hell was. Livin' with that ol' bat's disregard is no' even purgatory." She took a step away from Slims when she saw a man watching them curiously.

"Seems ye found a woman who interests ye at last, Slims," the man said with a chuckle.

Her gaze homed in on him, as she realized he was most likely a cousin. Where Sorcha was short and plump with reddish-brown hair, this man was tall and lean with thick blond hair in need of a trim. Even when not smiling, he always appeared to be on the verge of bursting into gales of laughter, and his brown eyes sparkled with merriment, although they held a hint of fatigue. She remembered the stationmaster mentioning a cousin who was a new father and wondered if this was Ewan. "Are ye Ewan?" she blurted out.

"Aye," he said with a quick smile. "Seems I'm famous." He winked at her.

"Ye have my trunk," she said.

"An' ye believe ye are Sorcha's cousin," he said, his tone cooling and his expression turning serious.

"I *am* her cousin. My da is a MacQueen." She nodded at the recognition of the name in his expression. "I ken ye were no' expectin' me to appear. But I'm here."

"Aye, ye are," Ewan said. "Come. Let's have you meet Jessie and Aileana." He pivoted, hopping off the boardwalk and reaching his arms up for her. After lifting her down, he offered his elbow. "Ye are a cousin of sorts, an' we've never been too particular about who we consider family. However, if ye hurt Sorcha, ye'll never be forgiven." He looked at her to see if she would agree.

"I understand. I have no intention of harming anyone," she said, "although there are times our actions have unforeseen consequences." She cast a glance over her shoulder and saw that Slims was following them.

"Aye, well said," Ewan murmured, as he squeezed her hand clasping his elbow. "Come. Jessie's bored with the snow an' men tryin' to create one tall tale after another. A cousin arrivin' in the middle of winter from Scotland will keep her entertained."

"Jessie?" Davina asked.

"My wife. She's the reporter in town. An' a fine one, although there is no' much to report." He winked at Davina. "Ye'll merit an article." Before she could protest, he led her up the steps of a fine house near the sheriff's. It was a row off the main street of town. "Jessie, I'm home with guests," he called out.

Davina tripped as she stared at a beautiful red-haired woman with hair falling loose, as she held a crying baby in her arms. Her rich cognac-colored eyes were filled with annoyance, although she attempted to hide it around a fleeting smile. "I can see 'tis a bad time. We canna stay."

"Oh, you're family," Jessamine said, as she heard Davina's accent. "You're very welcome. Aileana is fussy, and that makes me fussy." She passed the crying infant to Ewan, and he *coo*ed to his daughter, who continued to wail. However, soon she calmed and fell asleep in his arms.

"I have the magic touch," Ewan said with a smile, as he kissed the baby's downy black hair.

"Or she was exhausted and passed out," Slims said with a teasing grin. "Nice to see you, ma'am." He nodded his head deferentially to Jessamine and took off his hat.

Jessamine gazed from Slims to Davina. "You look the worse for wear. Come. Have a cup of tea or coffee."

"Actually, ma'am, I plan on goin' to the café and eatin'

everything they have on the menu," Slims joked. "We haven't eaten since yesterday."

Jessamine waved for them to follow her into the kitchen, where they were soon seated at the table. Jessamine poured them cups of coffee and cut up thick slabs of bread that she covered in butter. "Eat. Relax. And tell me what happened," she said, as she leaned forward with a reporter's avaricious gleam in her eyes.

"Jessie," Ewan said on a sigh. "Let 'em be."

"They're the most interesting thing to occur in the past month, Ewan MacKinnon. I'm not about to let this latest story just pass me by." She looked at Davina, who watched her with wide-eyed wonder. "I'm the reporter, and, although I might not always report what I hear, I long for stories. Please, tell me what happened to make you look like a pair of refugees."

"I feel like one in a borrowed dress," Davina said, "although I shouldna complain. I've been most fortunate in the friendship offered me by Sorcha and Frederick."

"And Slims," Ewan murmured with a wry quirk of his lips.

Slims kicked Ewan under the table and answered Jessamine's question. "We set out yesterday and were caught in the blizzard. We had to spend the night in one of the abandoned cabins a ways off the road."

"You could have frozen to death," Jessamine said.

"Aye we could have, but we had blankets we shared ..." Davina broke off with a flush and looked into her coffee cup, as her fingers played with crumbs on the tabletop.

"Shared?" Ewan asked with a roguish smile.

"You know as well as anyone we had to share body heat," Slims snapped. "Or you'd be looking for our carcasses today."

Jessamine fought a smile. "You know we're teasing. And we'd never want for you to suffer such an untimely death. Especially not now," she said cryptically, as she took a sip of her own coffee. "Tell me, Davina. How long do you plan to remain here in Bear Grass Springs?"

Davina's brows furrowed. "Long?" She cast a worried glance from Slims to Ewan. "I had hoped to settle here."

"Wonderful," Jessamine murmured, as she ran a hand down her slumbering daughter's back. She saw Slims watching her actions, and a contented smile bloomed. "We have a daughter, Slims," she said in a low voice.

"How?" he asked, flushing, as he blurted out the question. "I mean no disrespect, missus. I don't remember you being with babe the last time I was in town."

Jessamine laughed. "Heavens, no." She shared a loving look with her husband. "Ewan and I adopted little Aileana in December. She's the daughter of Ezekial and Beth, a Boudoir Beauty."

Slims jaw dropped open. "You adopted a Beauty's babe? Whyever for?"

"Do ye no' read Jessie's paper?" Ewan asked. "She wrote an eloquent article about it afore Christmas."

Shrugging, Slims said, "I must have missed it." After a moment, he asked, "Who's Ezekial?"

Ewan laughed. "Now ye're provin' just how good a man ye are. Ezekial was the doorman at the Boudoir. Kept out ruffians like me."

Slims stared at the couple in awe. "Remarkable."

"No reason a wee bairn should have to suffer for the folly of her parents," Ewan said, as he kissed his daughter's head. "An' we longed for a child." His reached his free hand out to Jessamine's, squeezing her hand before raising it to his lips for a kiss.

Davina swiped at her cheeks. "What's the Boudoir?"

"The bawdy house," Jessamine said. When Davina continued to stare at her in confusion, Jessie said, "The brothel. The house of ill repute. The ..."

"Enough, woman. We all ken ye're a walkin' thesaurus," Ewan said with exasperated fondness in his voice. "'Tis no' a place I want a cousin of mine to frequent, aye?" When Davina nodded, Ewan rose. "I'll lay her down for a wee rest. An' I'll show ye yer trunk."

A short time later, Davina knelt in front of the trunk she had packed with frantic haste as she clung to desperate hope that her life could be different with her cousin in Montana. She smiled as she saw the familiar dresses. Her fingers dug a little deeper, revealing the plaid in the MacDonald colors that had been her husband's. She continued to search through the trunk, until she touched the packet of letters she had sequestered away. With a sigh of relief, she relaxed. They had not gone missing.

"Is all well, lass?" Ewan asked. "I promise we did not root around in yer things." He shrugged and looked only mildly chagrined. "Well, Jessie forbade me to, an' I agreed. But it was no' for a lack of interest."

She laughed. "Ye are incorrigible, are ye no'?" When he merely shrugged, she pulled out the packet of letters. "I was worried these had gone astray."

"Are they letters from someone ye loved?" he asked.

"Aye," she whispered, her gaze distant. "But no' in the way ye mean. No' from my husband."

Ewan stood up straight. "What do ye mean, gallivantin' about the country with another man an' spendin' the night with him in a cabin if ye have a husband?"

She gazed at him until he calmed. "My husband's dead. I'm a widow." She traced a finger over the writing on the envelopes. "Nae, these are letters between my aunt Mairi an' yer da. An' between our two das." She held them to her chest, so Ewan couldn't yank them from her hold. "I wanted proof of who I am."

Swallowing a few times, Ewan took a deep breath. "Ye

70

have letters from Da? From my da?" At her nod, he whispered, "Could I see one?"

She bent her head, riffling through the letters until she found the one she wanted. "Here." She held the parchment out to him, watching as his hands shook as he gently gripped the fragile vellum. She watched as he slowly collapsed to his knees as his eyes raced over the words, his eyes filling with tears.

"Oh, Da," he whispered. "I wish I'd kent."

Davina stared at him with confusion.

"I did no' ken until a few years ago that Sorcha had a different mother. Which explained why my mother was always so cold and so cruel to her." He rubbed at his face. "Ye'll show this to Sorcha, aye? She still worries she is no' loveable."

Davina goggled at him. "How can she doubt? She has Frederick an' the bairns. An' the ranch hands would do anythin' for her."

Ewan rose and squeezed her shoulders. "Some hurts never fully heal, lass."

～

Slims tapped on the door to the room Davina had disappeared into, hoping she was awake and wanting a visitor. "Davina," he whispered.

"Aye," she said, creaking open the door. Her blond hair was tidily pulled back in a bun, and she wore a light-green dress that highlighted her subtle curves. She had tugged a shawl, made from a piece of tartan, over her shoulders, and he stood in awe of her.

"You've never looked more beautiful," he whispered. When she shook her head and looked down, he sighed. "Why will you not believe me when I speak the truth?" She did not raise her gaze, so he ceased pressing her for more than she was willing to offer. "Will you please come to the living room and talk with me, Davina?"

Her head jerked up at him using her name. "Yes, Simon," she whispered, sharing a private smile with him at the use of his first name.

He fought a chuckle and motioned for her to follow him. When they arrived in the sitting room, he sat in one of the high-backed chairs while she sat on the settee. The fire crackled, and they sat in quiet companionship for a few moments. "Ewan believes we should spend the night at Cailean's house, not the hotel. He said Cailean and Belle will be offended if we go to the hotel." He looked around the fine house. "Ewan worries we will be disturbed by their comings and goings as they worry about Aileana."

"Their comin' an' goin'?" Davina asked in confusion.

"It appears that Fidelia, Annabelle's sister, who just had a child in the fall, is ..." Slims waved his hand around, pointing to Davina's chest and stammering out incomprehensible sounds.

Davina sat in perplexed silence a moment before she blurted out, "Fidelia is breastfeedin' the bairn?"

"Yes," Slims said with a relieved sigh. "Yes, she is. No one else was available or willing to feed a Beauty's baby, and they knew she wouldn't thrive on powders."

Davina sat in contemplative silence as she stared at the fire. "What sort of family is this?"

Slims stiffened as he thought he detected a note of censure, rather than the true sense of wonder in her voice. "A family who looks out for each other," he said, "as they've looked out for you."

She gazed at him, her eyes shiny with unshed tears.

He froze, belatedly realizing he had misunderstood her. "Davina, there's no reason to cry."

"You dinna understand," she whispered. "For the majority of my life, I was raised to believe my aunt Mairi a horrible woman. A woman who had betrayed the sanctity of marriage and our family by lovin' a married man. An' that that man was the lowliest sort of man, whose family was never to be esteemed." She shook her head as a tear coursed down her cheek. "An' now I meet them, an' I realize they have more honor, more loyalty, more love one for the other than I ever kent. An' it breaks my heart." She rose, running to the room where her trunk was, the door shutting with a *thud* behind her.

"Dammit," Slims breathed.

Ewan emerged from the hallway and stared at Slims. "Whatever ye said did no' please the lass," he said with a wry smile, as he settled in front of the fire.

Swearing under his breath, Slims stared at the man he knew a little from Ewan's time visiting Sorcha, his sister, on the ranch. "Do we ever understand women?"

Ewan chuckled and shook his head. "Nae, but 'tis fun tryin' to." He looked at Slims. "Thank ye for ensurin' she was safe last night."

For a long moment, Slims was lost to the memory. To the sensation of holding Davina in his arms. "You have it backward, Ewan. She kept me safe. She ensured I didn't freeze to death." He let out a deep breath and shook his head, as though to clear it of memories. "Why are you and Jessamine living in Warren's house?" He looked around the fine home, known in town to be the lawyer, Warren Clark's, home. "I would have brought Davina to the wrong home to collect her trunk."

Ewan yawned and stretched before scratching at his head and sending his hair standing on end. "We swapped homes afore Christmas. Fidelia's helpin' us with Aileana, and we didn't want to be separated from our bairn during the months when she needed frequent feedin's." He yawned again. "I dinna ken what we would have done without Fidelia."

Slims stared at the younger man, struggling against deep-seated envy. "You are a lucky man, Ewan."

At Slims's whispered words, Ewan smiled. "Aye. I've a wife an' daughter and family around me. I could want for nothin' more." He stared at Slims. "Ye are no' alone either, Slims." His smile was cryptic. "An' I have a feelin' you'll be much less alone now than ye've ever been."

~

D avina walked beside Slims, as Ewan led the way on the short stroll to his eldest brother's house. Along the way, he jabbered about townsfolk, but she didn't pay much attention, as she had no idea who he talked about, assuming the chatter was for Slims's benefit, not hers. When they arrived at a large two-story house beside a livery with a paddock behind it, Ewan led them to a side entrance and ushered them into the kitchen.

Davina pressed into Slims's side, grateful she did not have to face this challenge alone. A tall man, his muscles rippling under his shirt, paced in the kitchen, although he was nowhere near as tall as Slims. An attractive black-haired woman of middling height sat at the table with a beautiful child on her lap. Unable to break her gaze from the child chattering away at her mother, Davina jerked when the man cleared his throat.

"So, you claim to be our cousin," the man said, his piercing eyes gleaming with mistrust.

She stiffened and forced herself to take a step away from Slims, although she remained near enough to reach out to touch his hand. "Aye, although ye are no' my cousin.

No' by blood. I'm Davina MacQueen. Yer sister is my cousin."

The man made a waving motion and shrugged. "If you're related to one MacKinnon, you're related to us all. We tend to be greedy when it comes to family. At least the Montana MacKinnons are." He studied her. "You're small, like Sorcha. And, from what Ewan told me, you're feisty like her too."

Davina raised her chin, as though daring him to disparage her.

"Who was your aunt?" the man asked. "What was she like?"

Davina let out a stuttering breath, the defiance leaving her. "Mairi?" she whispered. "Mairi was sweet an' kind an' good. She sang while she wove her cloth. An' she always had time to tell me a story or to teach me a song. She never thought I was a bother. An' she was never disappointed I was a girl." She ducked her head, as though embarrassed at having revealed too much.

"Aye, that sounds like Mairi." He smiled at her. "I met her a few times. I'm sorry I didn't know her better. But I believe we see all the goodness of Mairi in our wee Sorcha." He paused as he met her stunned gaze. "I'm Cailean, the eldest MacKinnon, an' I couldn't be happier you've come to find us, Davina." He tugged her into his arms, swallowing her squeak of surprise as he swung her around once and then set her on her feet again beside Slims. He beamed at Ewan. "We have another cousin."

Ewan smiled broadly. "Aye, we do, Cail."

"Annabelle's my wife, and Skye's our daughter," Cailean said with a proud smile.

"Skye," Davina whispered.

"Aye," he said, as he stared at his wife and daughter with delight. "She's our pride and joy."

"Why do ye no' talk like a Scot?" Davina blurted out.

Cailean laughed, pulling her close for a one-armed hug. "I worked hard to lose the accent when I arrived in America. I found I was treated better if I didn't sound like I was from a foreign land."

Ewan chuckled. "If ye make him angry, he'll sound like us." When she giggled, he winked at her.

Annabelle rose after Skye squirmed to be set on the ground. "I'm so glad we're finally meeting you," she said, as she pulled Davina close in a hug. "We'll have a family dinner tonight, and you can meet everyone." She shrugged. "Perhaps not everyone, but the majority of our family and those we consider family."

"I dinna wish to be a bother," Davina protested.

Annabelle shook her head. "Family is never a bother, Davina. We're delighted you're here." She saw Davina tracking Skye's movements with a wistful look in her gaze. "Would you like to hold her?"

"Oh, I wouldna presume ..." She broke off any protestations when Cailean hefted his daughter up and thrust Skye in Davina's arms. A smile burst forth as the girl beamed at her. "Hello. I'm your cousin Davina."

"Auntie," Skye murmured, as she sighed with contentment.

Davina stared in wonder at Annabelle and Cailean. "I'd think she'd be afraid of me."

Annabelle shrugged. "She goes through moments where she only wants me or Cailean. And then there are days, like today, when she wants to be held by anyone and everyone." She ran a hand down her daughter's back, laughing as her daughter giggled, as though being tickled.

When Skye began to squirm, Davina crouched and let her stand. Soon Skye had raced away to peer up at her uncle Ewan. When Davina noticed Annabelle watching her with an inquisitive look, she pasted on an impersonal smile. "Ye have a beautiful daughter."

"Aye," Annabelle murmured. "Thank you."

Davina sat at the crowded table, listening as the MacKinnons and those they considered family chattered around her. Slims sat to her right, and she gave thanks for his silent support. On her other side was a man named Bears, and he seemed content to watch the siblings laugh and tell stories, only imparting morsels of wisdom as needed. On the other side of Bears, the second-eldest MacKinnon brother, Alistair, sat beside his wife, Leticia. Continuing around the table, their eldest daughter, Hortence, whispered and giggled with Fidelia and Bears's daughter, Mildred. Ewan and Jessamine shared duties of caring for young Aileana, while another couple sat beside them. Fidelia sat between the unknown woman and Fidelia's sister, Annabelle, with Cailean next to Slims. Skye, Catriona, and Angus alternated between their parents' laps and playing on the floor.

"Ye have a beautiful son," Davina murmured to Bears in a lull in the conversation.

Bears nodded, his gaze moving to his wife, Fidelia, and their four-month-old son, with his chubby legs and cheeks, sitting on his mother's lap, smiling cheerfully at all those gathered. "He's a happy boy," he murmured. "My daughter, Bright Fawn, dotes on him, as do we all." He nodded to a girl at the table—who looked like him, with dark hair and deep brown eyes—who Davina had also heard called Mildred. Slims had warned her that Bears had more than one name for most people.

"Ye are very blessed," she whispered.

He stared at Davina a long moment and nodded. "Yes, I

am." He looked deeply into her eyes, and she found herself unable to look away from his penetrating gaze. "I fear you believe you have not been so blessed."

She shrugged and cleared her throat as she fought tears. "I've never been one to inspire loyalty. Or love."

Bears stared at her in wonder, a soft smile playing around his lips. "I fear you've believed other's truths for too long. You must learn to recognize what you know to be true and to not accept the falsehoods others feed you."

Davina sat in silence, wringing her fingers together on her lap, as she watched the MacKinnons laugh and chatter around her. "How can you know this?"

Bears followed her gaze. "Already you've inspired the MacKinnons to extend their hospitality to you." He shook his head as she was about to protest. "They don't have gatherings like this for just anyone." He paused. "You've survived weeks on the ranch with Sorcha. Which means, she considers you friend, if not family. If you are brave enough to accept what they offer you, Davina, you will have a full, happy life here."

Davina broke off what more she might have said when Ewan called her name. "Aye?" she asked him. Already she considered him cousin.

"I want ye to meet Ben Metcalf and his beautiful wife, Jane," Ewan said, as he nodded to the unknown couple. "Ben's my right-hand man, an' Jane's Frederick's cousin." He beamed at his friend. "We're officially family, which means I receive a discount at the Waterin' Hole."

Frowning, Davina shook her head in confusion, as Ben laughed at Ewan's joke. "Waterin' Hole?"

Jane, a beautiful brown-haired woman, who glowed under her husband's devoted attention, flushed beet red. "It's a saloon in town. Ben and I own it."

"Truly?" Davina asked.

"She won it in a bet," Ben said with pride, as his hand

played with loose strands of hair on Jane's shoulder. "Out-smarted an inveterate gambler."

"Oh my," Davina whispered.

"Aye," Ewan said with a chuckle. "She won a more valuable asset than ever's been bet in any gamblin' match in town."

"Except for Fidelia," Bears murmured.

"Of course," Ewan said, with a wink to his sister-in-law. "But Dee is, an' never was, somethin' to be bartered."

"We're only fortunate that the Madam was desperate to continue her play and that you won," Annabelle said.

Davina sat in wide-eyed wonder, as her extended family discussed gambling as readily as the women on the Isle of Sky did their favorite church hymns. Davina relaxed when Slims gripped her hand and squeezed it.

"They find a way to take what has hurt them, or has the potential to hurt them, and turn it into a story that entertains. It removes any potential poison and binds them closer together," he whispered into her ear.

"'Tis remarkable," she breathed. "I've never seen anythin' like it."

"Well, this is what *family* means to them. Even if you're no blood relation, if they take a likin' to you, you're a member." As the kitchen door was thrust open, and an elderly couple entered, Slims rose abruptly, dropping her hand. "Mister, missus," he said in a deferential, near-reverent tone.

"We've come to meet the woman who claims she's family," the older man said. He appeared to be in his midseventies, with thick gray hair, slightly stooped shoulders, and an intelligent gaze.

The woman jabbed him in his side, her astute gaze homing in on Davina. Her dress had seen its share of washes, but she held herself proudly, and her gray hair was tied back in a knot at her nape. "Welcome. You've had a long journey, but we hope you will feel as at home here as in Scotland."

Davina rose and nodded to them, fighting an urge to curtsy to the couple, although she had never curtsied to anyone. "Thank ye," she said in a quivering voice, as she fought a sudden onslaught of nerves. Everyone at the table had quieted to watch this introduction. "I am Davina MacQueen, and I'm Sorcha's cousin."

"*Davina*," the man said with a pleased sigh. "What a beautiful name. Now how are you related to our Sorcha?"

Standing tall, Davina said, "Her mother, Mairi, was my aunt."

"Mairi," Harold said with a nod. "'Bout time someone from your family showed sense and came lookin' for Sorcha. She's a jewel." He rounded the table and pulled Davina into a hug. "Welcome."

Squeaking with surprise, Davina didn't react in time to embrace him before he released her.

The older woman approached with a chagrined smile. "Forgive Harold. He's lost any manners he ever had." She reached forward and squeezed Davina's hand. "We're Irene and Harold Tompkins. Frederick's grandparents."

"Oh, how lovely," Davina breathed, before she could stop herself. She flushed as she heard chuckles from everyone at the table.

"Yes, it sure is," Harold said with a self-satisfied grin. "It means, if you're related to Sorcha, you're related to us too." He nodded as though there were no more logic to work through.

Irene squeezed Davina's hand again. "No point arguing, dear. Once he's taken you under his wing, you're there forever."

"Oh, how lovely," Davina whispered again, now battling tears.

"Come. None of this," Irene said, pulling her forward in a soft embrace. She held Davina, murmuring about imagining being overwhelmed at meeting them all. "And we run the local café, so you must come visit. You are always welcome."

Davina laughed when she heard Harold say, "I hope we're not too late for dessert. No one bakes a better cake than you, Anna."

Davina raised her head and met Irene's amused stare. "Do ye no' mind him sayin' that?"

Irene shrugged. "Anna makes the best cakes from here to Helena, if not in the Territory. I can't fault my husband for being truthful." She spoke softly, so only Davina would hear, "But I would protest if he likes anyone's fried chicken more than mine."

Davina giggled, and Irene winked at her. Soon Irene had urged Davina back to the table, where the stories and the laughter continued.

Davina tossed and turned. After punching her pillow for the fifteenth time, she rolled onto her back and sighed, as she stared at the ceiling. Sleep would not come to her. Snippets from the day played over and over in her mind, and she marveled at her family. At their generosity. At their use of humor to show love and affection, rather than to hurt or to show one's perceived superiority. At the frequent laughter, hugs, and expressions of joy. How different they were from her own family. From anyone in her husband's family.

She heard a creaking in the hallway and assumed Slims had risen to pilfer Annabelle's well-stocked larder. Rubbing her stomach, she debated the merits of seeking out another piece of cake and decided she'd eaten her fill.

As the door to her room opened with the merest squeak, she gasped. Rather than tiptoe downstairs, Slims stood staring in at her. Yanking the sheets and blankets up to her chin, she gasped, "What are ye doin'?"

He smiled, his gaze roving over her. "Checking on you. Ensuring you are well." He saw the bedsheets torn from the bed, and his smile broadened. "Seems you are having as restless a night as I. May I?"

She paused a long moment, their gazes locked together before she whispered, "Aye."

He slipped inside, shutting the door with a barely audible *click*. He wore the same clothes he'd worn into town, although they were now dry, albeit very rumpled. "May I lie on top of the covers while you fall asleep?" he asked, as he stood beside her bed.

"Nae."

"Davina, I promise—" His words broke off when she gripped his hand and squeezed it.

"Nae, Simon. I want ye to hold me. Make me feel safe again. Cherished," she whispered.

He groaned, falling to his knees, so he was at eye level with her. "I don't want you to feel forced into letting me into your bed."

She giggled. "I'm only askin' ye to hold me, ye ken?"

He traced a finger over her smiling cheek. "I know," he whispered. "And that's much more than I ever thought I'd have."

Davina scooted over, holding the blankets up so he could slide into the place she'd occupied. When he'd settled, she rested her head on his shoulder. Quiet night sounds settled over them. The faint crescendo and decrescendo of a snore. The soft whistling of the wind. The distant yipping of coyotes.

His fingers traced up and down her arm, while his head

arched over her, so he could kiss her soft hair. "Why are you still tense?" He spoke in a low voice, so Cailean and Annabelle wouldn't wake and hear them, discovering him in her room. "If having me here brings you more distress, I'll leave."

She gripped his arm, rubbing her face against his cotton-covered chest. "Nae, stay. Please."

"On all that is holy, I wish I were as I was last night," he muttered, earning a startled gasp from her, as she recalled he had been as naked as the day he was born. He kissed her hair again and relaxed against the pillows, continuing to run his hands over her. With every caress, every soft word of praise, she relaxed incrementally more.

"I worry about church tomorrow," she said, as she turned to press her face into his neck, as though attempting to hide against him. She breathed deeply of his scent—a mixture of soap, horses, and a musky scent that she knew was all Slims. Without a thought, she kissed him there, earning a shiver.

"*Shh*, darlin'," Slims soothed, forcing himself to focus on what she said, not her actions. "Your cousins are good people. As are the Tompkinses. Trust them. They would never intentionally hurt you."

She rested her head against his chest. "I've only kent them a day, but I believe ye." She shivered. "It's the preacher I dinna trust. I ken they said he would no' act out on his last day, but still I worry."

"You have people you can rely on, Davina."

She traced fingers down his arm, until she reached his hand, intertwining her fingers with his. "I missed this," she murmured, as sleep beckoned.

"What?" he asked.

"These moments of quiet sharin'. Of consolin' and carin', when nothin' more was expected. When disappointment and anger werena all I felt."

"I'll never feel that way about you, Davina," Slims vowed.

"So ye say," she whispered, her words slowing, as she neared sleep. "But I ken things change. An' never for the better."

"Davina," he whispered, but he heard her breath deepening, as though she were about to fall asleep.

"Roll over," he whispered. He helped turn her gently to her side and tugged her back to his front, cocooning her with his large body. He tugged the blankets around them and held her securely to him. "There, love."

"*Love*," she murmured. "I've never been anyone's love." She tumbled into sleep, leaving Slims with jumbled thoughts beside her.

CHAPTER 5

Slims sat beside Davina, yearning to hold her hand, but aware that it was wholly inappropriate in church. The MacKinnon family filled the rows in front, beside, and behind him, and he took comfort in the fact he was not alone for the pastor's last sermon. Although Harold and Irene had urged them to attend, Slims worried their presence would prove a grave mistake. Now, in the light of day, he dreaded having Davina's fears come to life.

His mind was filled with her. Of holding her in his arms. Of their short talk before she fell asleep. Of waking with her again cradled to his chest, where he always wished she'd be. Of hearing her small noises as she woke and of kissing her forehead. Of letting go of all worries as she cuddled into him, rather than forcing him from her bed and her room. Of meeting Cailean's concerned gaze as Slims slipped from her room, and the silent nod from the eldest cousin signaling he trusted Slims.

He focused on his surroundings and noted the large attendance for the pastor's last sermon, before Pastor Cruik-shanks departed Bear Grass Springs. When Slims felt Davina shiver next to him, her murmured, "Don't worry. You aren't alone here, and you'll never be alone again."

She placed her hand on her lap, her fingers inching toward his, so that her pinkie finger touched his.

"Ah, miss," he whispered, "how you please me." He quieted as the pastor entered, and the congregation stood.

After they sang a hymn, everyone sat, and Pastor Cruikshanks strode to the front of the church. He stepped up to the pulpit, his long black robes flowing around him. He outstretched his arms to those worshipping with him that day, although it appeared as though he were summoning a curse rather than a benediction. He did not reach for his Bible to read a verse and then discuss it, as was his custom.

Instead his beady eyes were lit with a fervent righteousness, and he raised one hand with a finger pointing to the ceiling. "Jezebel," he said in a loud, precise voice. "A Jezebel is among us, and we must do everything in our power to rid ourselves of temptation."

The parishioners squirmed, casting nervous, embarrassed glances at each other. Men cast relieved glances, as they knew they wouldn't be the focus of the pastor's wrath. The women patted at their hair and skirts, anxious that they were not the one to be called out by the preacher. For all knew they had sinned in one way or another. None were without blemish.

The pastor slammed his hand down on the wooden pulpit, causing those tittering and fidgeting to jump and to focus on him. "She is a charmer. Speaks with a forked tongue, appearing beguiling and innocent, when, in reality, she is wanton and wicked. Rather than join her brethren in the house of sin, sparing the townsfolk from her lascivious wiles, only sullying the reputations of those so-called gentlemen foolish enough to enter a house of ill-repute, she tricked God-fearing men to bring her to a ranch. Thus turning such an estimable place into its own den of iniquity."

Slims glowered at the pastor, his breath coming in near pants as he fought his rage. He cast a glance at Davina, and she sat beside him with her hands gripped together in her lap, and her head lowered, as though in shame. He raised wrathful eyes to stare at the pastor, as the man continued his diatribe.

"For who among us could ever resist the call of a Jezebel?" Pastor Cruikshanks asked, his face red and splotchy, a spot of spittle on his chin. "Who among us has the strength to deny her when she taunts and teases us with her libidinous wiles?"

By this point, Slims had stiffened with righteous anger and was on the verge of attacking the pastor, holy man or not.

However, Alistair sat on his other side and kept a firm hand on his thigh. "Dinna even consider it," Alistair whispered.

"Everyone in this town believes the MacKinnons to be a respectable, honorable family. Taking in strays. Building successful businesses." The pastor scoffed and rocked on his feet, as though the mere suggestion of honor or decency with relation to the MacKinnons were a mockery of the word.

"You tell me. Which marriage among the siblings wasn't tinged by scandal? Which marriage didn't have an element of shame or regret associated with it?" he roared. "Too often they didn't even believe in the sanctity of a marriage in front of this fine congregation. No, our blessing was not needed. Only the blessing of their family and friends. And now, now, they have welcomed in the worst woman yet."

He shook his head, as he leaned on the pulpit, as though his strength had left him at such a notion. "Now they are forcing you, you my wonderful Christian brethren, so filled with charity and goodwill, to suffer the presence of such a woman. A woman who would spend the night with a man while unmarried. And feels no compunction!" he roared, his arms waving about, as though he were in the midst of a fit.

"Right," Slims muttered. "I've had enough."

"Aye," Alistair said. He muttered something, and the MacKinnon family stood up as one, along with Harold and Irene Tompkins, Warren and Helen Clark, Leena and Karl Johansen, and Ben and Jane Metcalf. Over one-quarter of the congregants moved to depart en masse.

With Davina in the middle, they turned for the door, the pastor's raging and abuse raining down on them. However, they moved without haste, as though they were impervious to his words. Their calm retreat seemed to enrage Pastor Cruikshanks even more, as the volume of his vitriol rose.

Finally, at the door, Harold Tompkins turned around and yelled back, "Cruiks, you may believe you used your pulpit well. You may believe sowing your seeds of dissension and hate were a worthwhile way to spend your Sundays. You may believe allowin' your jealousy and your envy to eat away at you was a good way to while away your life. But it wasn't, and it ain't." Harold glared at the man who'd been in town for years, using Harold's family as a bludgeon every time he was in a sore mood. "Your cross to bear is that you'll never fully understand friendship or familial love. You'll perpetually wonder why such basic sentiments as love and loyalty will forever be denied you. And I'll know that my prayers are answered and that God is good on the day I watch your wagon roll out of town." He glared at the pastor before turning on his heel, slamming the door behind him and the awestruck congregation.

~

A blinding sun glinted off the bright snow, and they paused outside the church. Davina shook in stunned silence, as the pastor's muffled voice could be heard bellowing inside. Thankfully they could not make out his words.

"Come," Annabelle whispered. "Come to the house, and we'll have tea and a treat. Everything is better with a treat." She slung an arm over Davina's shoulder, sending a worried glance to Slims.

Slims watched Annabelle and Davina depart, wishing he could offer her comfort, but knowing such an action would only engender more gossip. He stood with his hands fisted and arms quivering, as though readying for battle. "If I ever see that man again …" he rasped, as he imagined how Davina suffered.

Cailean gripped his shoulder. "Hopefully you won't. He leaves on the train tomorrow. And none of us will be stupid enough to tell you where he's going."

Ewan looked at his brothers. "No one should be stupid enough to tell any of us where he's goin'," he snapped. "Did ye hear how he criticized all of us in there?"

Jessie looped her arm through Ewan's. "Never fear. He's given me the most entertaining material for an article that I've had in months. I'm quite looking forward to writing it." Her beautiful eyes sparkled with mischief. For once, no one was urging her to temper her wit, which could be savage.

As Slims suspected, the MacKinnon men relaxed and laughed. However, Slims remained tense. "I can't abide that he spoke against her in such a way."

Helen squeezed his arm. "You know he heard the rumors from my mother, who was only too happy to spread her lies." Her gaze glowed with regret and embarrassment. "I'm sorry, Slims. I'm sorry she continues to hurt those I care about."

"You have nothin' to apologize for, Miss Helen," Slims murmured, the tension finally seeping away from him, as he saw how his anger was affecting those he cared about.

Cailean motioned for them to walk across the street to his home. "Come. I don't want to be here when the congregants leave." He slung an arm over Harold's shoulder. "Besides, 'tis time to raise a glass to Harold. Who would have thought he'd speak out in church against the pastor?"

Harold laughed and shook his head. "I fear you will think me a fool," he muttered to his wife.

Irene, who walked beside him, squeezed his arm. "I will not. I couldn't be prouder," she said. "It wasn't a young whippersnapper who put that man in his place, but you, you irascible old goat." Her eyes shone with pride.

Slims smiled at the older couple he'd known since he was a young man. He'd arrived in Fort Benton, penniless and broken in every way. For some reason, Harold had taken him under his wing, and, when they left Fort Benton to homestead land in Bear Grass Springs, Slims had traveled with them. He'd learned everything he knew about ranching and horses from Harold and his son. More important, Slims had been accepted into their family and had learned to believe in loyalty again. "Thank you, sir," he murmured to Harold, as he walked on Harold's other side.

"Don't you *sir* me, Slims," Harold muttered. "You're as much family as any of 'em." He nodded to the MacKinnon brothers, laughing and tossing snowballs at each other. "And I know you'll do what must be done."

Slims sighed and nodded. "Yes, sir."

Harold paused outside of Cailean's house and spoke in a low, sincere voice. "And you'll refrain from any violence as Pastor Cruikshank performs the ceremony." He waited with blatant amusement glowing in his gaze, as Slims swore silently.

"Yes, Mr. Harold. I will."

"There's a good lad," Harold said. "Come. Miss Annabelle makes the best coffee." He gasped as Irene belted him on his arm. "Well, she does, Ireney. I can't help but speak the truth."

"Don't let your success with the pastor go to your head, you old coot," she muttered. "Or you'll be sleeping on a cot."

Slims chuckled, following them into Cailean's house. He wished he was as free of worry as they were. For he had to find a way to convince Davina to marry again. Tonight.

~

D avina sat in the kitchen with the women, while the men lounged in the living room. Annabelle, Leticia, and Fidelia fluttered around the stove, while Jessamine, Helen, and she sat with a child on their laps. Davina held Catriona, Alistair and Leticia's daughter, who was a little over one year old. Helen held Jack, Fidelia and Bears's baby boy, and Jessamine held her daughter, Aileana.

Conversation flowed around her, as the women told Fidelia what had occurred in church that morning. Once Fidelia was up to date with the morning's adventure, Davina attempted to join the conversation or to pay attention to learn more about town, but she sat in a dazed stupor as the pastor's words continued to ring in her ears.

"Davina?" Annabelle asked again. She had sat beside her and now held her three-year-old daughter, Skye, in her lap. "Are you well?"

Davina shook her head and shrugged. "I dinna ken." She saw Fidelia and Leticia share a smile and frowned. "What did I say that was humorous?"

Fidelia pulled out a chair and sat with a sigh of relief. "Nothing, and it was rude of me. But you remind me so much of Sorcha, and I miss her desperately. Hearing you speak eases that ache."

Davina stared at the women seated around her in wonder. "I dinna understand ye, any of ye." She rubbed at her head. "The pastor warned ye to stay away from me. That I'm a ... a ...." Her voice broke as she was unable to even whisper the word *Jezebel*.

Leticia laughed, accepting a squirming Catriona, and settled her on her lap as she sat down too. "If you're one, so are we all." She nodded as Davina gaped at her. "Belle was caught kissing Cailean and had to marry him or face the town's wrath, even though she could barely stand him. I broke Alistair's heart as my not-dead first husband interrupted our first wedding and nearly ruined our relationship. Jessamine's father almost tore off the church door in an attempt to prevent her wedding to Ewan."

"Would have only been an improvement for the church," Jessamine muttered as she made faces at Aileana.

Leticia raised an eyebrow at her sister-in-law, as she continued to tick off all the ways the women of the family had had unconventional marriages or wedding ceremonies. "Helen was forced to marry Warren after spending time on the ranch."

"I wasn't forced. I chose to," Helen interjected. "Although there was the matter of the virgin auction at the Boudoir."

All of the women laughed as Davina leaned forward, as though eager to hear that story. When Helen whispered, "I'll tell you later," Davina sighed with frustration.

Leticia continued. "Leena's marriage wasn't a scandal, more's the pity. But Sorcha's was, having to marry after two men slept in her bedroom, when she was bedbound at the ranch after she broke her leg."

"What?" Davina asked, her gaze widening in astonishment.

Annabelle laughed. "Yes, you should have seen our husbands." That sent the women into gales of laughter.

When they had calmed down, Fidelia smiled smugly. "Bears and my marriage wasn't scandalous. Everyone in town was excited for our marriage."

"Everyone but the Madam," Jessamine muttered, earning a gasp from Davina.

Fidelia flushed and then shrugged. "Yes, there's the small matter that I used to work at the Boudoir."

"And finally there's Jane. Who had to marry Ben because her brother had bet her in a gambling match," Leticia said triumphantly. "You'd be following a wonderful family tradition."

Davina gaped at the women and then paled, her eyes rounded with shock and horror. "Ye think I'm marryin'? No, never again."

"Never's a long time, and I hear the pastor is to call tonight. It would be a delicious irony if he were to marry you after today's sermon," Jessamine said, as she took a sip of tea. "A perfect ending to my story." She paused as she saw the true panic in Davina's gaze. "Although we had unconventional courtships and marriages, we all found love, Davina. Slims is a good man."

Davina sat frozen in her chair. She closed her eyes in despair. "I did no' want to marry out of duty or desperation. I wanted more," she whispered. "Why could that man no' let us be?" She sniffled and pulled out a handkerchief to swipe at her nose. "Why did I have to say anythin' to that horrid woman yesterday?"

Helen flushed and ducked her head. "I'm sorry, Davina. My mother thrives on causing discord and unhappiness."

"She's yer mother?" Davina asked. "How is that possible?" She looked at the other women. "Ye astound me."

Annabelle kissed Skye's head. "Why? Because we accept

Helen so readily into our group?" Annabelle shook her head, arching her head away as Skye tried to pull at an earring. "Helen's one of us, and she shouldn't have to suffer for the sins of her mother any more than Aileana should."

"Or Sorcha," Fidelia said.

"No," Davina agreed. "Auntie Mairi was a good woman. A wonderful aunt." She met their intense gazes, filled with interest. "She was my favorite, of anyone in my family. The best storyteller an' she taught me the most beautiful songs." Davina looked down. "I miss her still."

Annabelle smiled. "So you understand. Not everyone in our family can be as we wish they were." She shared a look with her sister, Fidelia. "Our father was a miserly, miserable man, who thrived on making everyone around him as unhappy as he was."

Fidelia shivered. "I'll never mourn that he's dead."

Jessamine tapped the table. "You're moving away from the issue at hand. Davina must marry. And she needs to marry Slims."

"I dinna want to marry due to the preacher's bullyin' from his pulpit," Davina protested.

Helen reached forward and gripped her hand. "Don't you like Slims? He was always one of my favorites at the ranch." She smiled when she saw a flash of jealousy in Davina's gaze. "I lived at the ranch for a little over a month, after Warren and I fought. Warren didn't realize I was a midwife and didn't understand why I would disappear at night. Frederick offered me a place to go."

"How are ye all so good?" Davina blurted out.

Fidelia's gaze was filled with compassion. "I too had trouble believing our friends and family could be so generous, with no hope for a favor in the future. But that's who they are, Davina. Who we are." She reached forward and took Davina's other hand. "Who you are too."

"Marry Slims and be one of us," Leticia urged, before grimacing. "I know you are already because you're Sorcha's cousin, but, if you marry Slims, you'll live on the ranch, and we'll see you at town dances. You'll never have a reason to leave."

Davina sat in silence, fighting tears. "I dinna ken. I have to speak with Slims first."

Annabelle nodded. "As you should. Every woman wants a proper proposal."

Slims entered the kitchen, pausing as he saw the women seated around the table, laughing and talking. His breath caught at the sight of Davina giggling at something Jessamine said, Skye on her lap, her cheeks flushed and her eyes filled with joy. He stood, staring his fill, wanting to remember this moment forever. For he knew, in this moment, that he would never doubt wanting her to be his wife.

He was fond of her, yearned for her to always be safe, and desired her. His mind instinctively shied away from the word *love*, but he knew he had never cared for a woman as he did her, not since he was a young man. He smiled as the conversation stilled as his presence was noted. Disappointment and nerves filled him when he saw trepidation in Davina's gaze.

"I didn't mean to interrupt your gathering," he said in his deep baritone, "but I had hoped I could speak with Davina."

Davina watched him wide-eyed, not saying anything.

"The house is near bursting with family," he continued. "I thought I could show Davina the livery and introduce her to my favorite horses here."

"Yes, just what a woman wants. To meet more horses,"

Jessamine muttered. Someone else snickered, but Davina rose.

"Yes, Slims, thank ye." After she'd bundled into her coat, they walked the short distance from the house to the livery. Inside, it was comfortably warm, although not nearly as warm as the inviting kitchen with the stove pumping out heat. Davina strode ahead of him, walking toward the first horse that had its head sticking out of a stall.

"That's Brindle," Slims said. "He's as docile as they come." He watched as she patted the horse, giving him a good scratch behind his ears. "He's Alistair's horse."

She made a noncommittal sound, moving farther into the livery. When she reached the tack room, she poked her head inside. "I've never seen one so organized."

Slims chuckled. "That would be Bears. He's a genius with horses and likes to keep the tack room tidy." He walked toward her, pausing when he saw her tense as he neared. "Davina, ignore what the preacher said. Remember last night."

Her brown eyes glowed in the lantern light, like the richest of chocolates, as the stiffness in her shoulders eased the longer she stared into his eyes. "Thank ye for soothin' my nerves."

He took a step toward her. "Is that all it was to you?" His gaze searched hers. "Me soothing your nerves?"

She took a deep breath and stepped nearer to him. "Of course no'." She reached up, her hand cupping his cheek, as her eyes filled with tears. "I wanted time, Slims."

His eyes closed at her soft touch. "Time?" he whispered, as he rested his hands on her hips, holding her close, but still giving her the freedom to back away from his embrace at any moment.

"Time to feel free," she choked out.

He opened his eyes. "I would never mean for you to feel caged by me," he whispered.

"Whether you mean it or not, 'twill happen." She traced a finger down an oiled piece of leather. "I know almost nothin' about you. How can we marry?"

Slims saw a stool in the corner and pulled it out, sitting down, so he no longer towered over her. "What would you know?"

"Where are ye from? Who are yer people?" She stared deeply into his brown eyes. "Why have ye no' married? Ye must be in yer forties." Her brows crinkled, as though flummoxed that he was unwed.

Rather than laugh her off or attempt to make light of her questions, he gazed at her with a sober introspection. He tugged over another stool and motioned for her to sit. "If you want to know, then listen." At her nod, he let out a deep breath. "I was born in Kansas, and, like most from that fine state, I worked on a farm with my parents and siblings. We knew hard times, but my parents were good people. Intent on providing a better life for their children. But hard times were coming for us. Kansas was a violent place when I was a young man. My pa wanted peace. Didn't want to take sides in the debate of the day." He sighed and rubbed his head. "But, in the end, he had to."

"I dinna understand," Davina whispered.

"Kansas was a territory, like Montana, and the people were votin' to decide if it would be a state that supported slavery or not. My pa finally made his opinion known—that he was against slavery—and he was killed for it."

"Oh, Simon," she whispered.

He stared in the distance. "I was young and a fool. I'd taken a shine to a young woman, and I had trusted her with my pa's belief. With my own." He shook his head and sat in silence for a few moments, the only sounds that of the horses shifting in their stalls. "Damn fool." His muscles tautened under his shirt. "She told her father, a proslavery man, and a mob came to the house."

"What happened?" she whispered, holding his large hand between her two smaller ones.

His gaze was distant for a moment, before he focused on her again, this time filled with shame. "Even though I was such a young man, I was a good fighter. And my pa knew few would challenge us, as long as I was nearby. I was a giant of a man, even then." He sighed. "But I was also a young man, desirous of love and affection."

He shook his head at his folly. "A woman about my age caught my eye. She was demure in what she wore but had the boldness to meet my gaze. Few did, as my size intimidated them. Soon we talked and sent letters. Secret messages. Secret meetings near the house. One night I was a fool and allowed her to entice me away from the house." He flushed. "Little did I know her task had been to waylay me and to attempt to kill me. She failed on the killing-me part."

He let out a raspy breath. "When I returned home, my family was dead. All of them. Even little Johnny, only two years old. Killed by the mob who came while I was away from the house." He stared into space, as though reliving that horrific night. "Her people wanted to make sure no one against slavery held property or lived in the area. And they wanted our land. They had connections with the sheriff, who approved of slavery, so no charges were ever filed."

Bitterness twisted his mouth. "Turns out, she was praised for not killin' me. As I was the only living member of my family, suspicion fell to me, and I was shunned by everyone who I had thought friend. Overnight I had no family, an' I was an outsider in the only place that had ever been home. The sheriff advised me to leave and to forfeit my family's land or to suffer as they had." He swiped a palm over his mouth and ducked his head. "I was a coward, Davina. I ran. As far as I could. I drifted for years. And found the Tompkins family in Fort Benton."

"Oh, Simon," she whispered. "It was no' your fault. Ye have to ken, if ye'd been home, the mob would have killed ye too. That is the nature of mobs, aye? No matter what yer da said, yer presence could no' have saved anyone, not even ye." She stared into his eyes but saw the futility of her argument.

He stared at her with impotent fury and self-hatred. "I was a fool for a woman, and my family paid the price. Tell me. Who else is to blame?" He bit his lip. "I swore, on everything and everyone I ever loved, I would never repeat that mistake again. I would never allow a woman to mar my judgment and to threaten all I love." He paused for a long moment, as his gaze roved over her. "I worried I had, with you."

She took a deep breath, her hand dropping from his, shock and hurt in her gaze. "I'd never do such a thing." Her gaze darted in the direction of the house, where her family laughed and told stories. "I'd never harm them."

"I believe you now. I wasn't so certain when you arrived, with your secrets and your unwillingness to tell the whole truth." He half smiled, as though he were a young man, embarrassed at sitting so near the woman he fancied. "No woman intent on wreaking havoc would have fought as hard as you did to keep me alive and warm."

She flushed.

"I will never forget the memory of you holding my feet to your chest."

"Slims," she admonished, holding her fingers over his lips, before dropping her hand to clench his again.

He laughed, staring deeply into her eyes. After a long moment, he sobered. "I'm older than you think, Davina, and I hope that doesn't make you wish for a younger man." He

99

smiled as her grip on his hand tightened. "I'm fifty-one. I'll be fifty-two in March." He raised his head to gaze into her earnest face. "Rather too old for a jewel like you."

"Nae," she whispered. "I'm nearly forty. I've no need of a young husband who will want things from me I canna give him."

"Children?" Slims whispered. At her nod, he cupped her cheek. "I never expected to marry. I thought the children I would adore would be Frederick's and his brothers'. My soul does not call out for them." He paused. "But it does for you."

Her eyes widened at his whispered admission. "Simon," she breathed. "I ... I fear yer eventual disappointment in me. That ye will come to wish I were somethin' other than I am." She closed her eyes in defeat. "An' I fear I couldna bear it a second time."

Cupping her cheek, Slims leaned forward, brushing a featherlight kiss to her soft skin as he breathed into her ear. "I am not him. Let me prove that to you."

"I fear I dinna have the courage." A tear coursed down her cheek.

"I know you do," he murmured. "How brave you were, to defy your father and to travel all the way from Scotland. And then to attempt to walk to the ranch from town in the middle of winter." His fingers stroked her cheek. "And then to fight to prevent me from freezing to death." He kissed the side of her neck. "You have all the courage you'll ever need, but you must have faith in it. And in yourself."

She leaned forward and would have tumbled off the stool if he hadn't caught her and tugged her onto his lap. "I'm too heavy," she protested.

"Ah, love, that's the joy of marryin' such a giant like me." He wrapped his arms around her, breathing in the soft fragrance of soap, cinnamon, and a scent that was all her. "Trust me." He eased away, any levity or teasing absent from his gaze as he stared earnestly into her eyes. "I will never be the owner of a fine ranch. But I am loyal and honest and true. And I promise you, Davina, if you marry me, I will do everything I can to ensure you never feel small or belittled by me. Instead I want you to feel cherished and adored. You will be my wife, and you will be respected."

He paused, knowing the words a woman longed to hear had been omitted from his passionate speech. However, he refused to lie to her, and he would not say what he was terrified of feeling. "Will you marry me?"

She gazed deeply into his eyes and then nodded. "Yes, I'll marry ye, Simon."

He let out a *whoop* and leaned forward, kissing her passionately. He groaned as her fingers dug into his shoulders, holding him as close as he held her. His hands sank into her soft hair, loosening the strands, although not enough to have the golden locks tumble down her back.

He broke the kiss and held her against his chest. "Soon, my darlin', soon," he whispered in her ear.

A voice clearing in the livery had Slims looking over his shoulder, as he kept her in his protective embrace. "Yes?"

Bears poked his head into the tack room. "The preacher will be here in half an hour, and the ladies want to ensure Davina has time to prepare for the ceremony."

Slims released her, when she pushed against his chest, his irritation at being denied holding her fading when she kissed his jaw and whispered, "Soon." With a soft stroke down her back, he steadied her on her feet and then rose to watch her scurry back to the house. Somehow he knew his life would never be the same.

A soft wind had picked up again, as it had the previous night. Few ventured outside in the frigid temperatures, but Slims had a need to be out of doors for a few minutes. Away from the hustle and bustle inside, as they awaited the arrival of the preacher. Bears stood beside Slims on the back porch, while the women fussed inside over Davina.

"*Simon?*" Bears murmured, a hint of amusement in his voice.

"Don't even," Slims warned.

Bears chuckled, his gaze friendly and filled with compassion. "You do realize you'll have to use your real name with the preacher? And then they'll all find out?" Bears shook his head, his long black hair swaying slightly with the movement. "And then you'll never have any peace as they tease you."

Slims rubbed at his temple. "I don't know what to do."

Sobering in an instant, Bears stood tall, as he studied the ranch hand he knew only a little. "You don't have to marry. Another scandal will come along soon, and the preacher is leaving tomorrow. He won't have the chance to spread any more vicious lies about you or Davina. And, if there is any justice in this world, the new preacher will have more compassion."

Slims shook his head. "You know what it's like. I'll be exonerated because I'm a man. She'll have to live with a black cloud over her head forever. Simply because she was too kindhearted to let me freeze." He stared out at the night's sky.

"Call me a fool," Bears said, a hint of irony in his voice, as few would ever be so witless as to call him that, "but I thought you genuinely cared for her."

"I do," Slims whispered, "but I fear it won't be enough."

Bears moved so he leaned against the railing and faced the larger man. Light from inside the kitchen glinted off his face, highlighting his high cheekbones and darker skin, a testament to his Native American mother. "What are you afraid of?" When Slims remained silent, Bears murmured, "I was afraid of losing my freedom. And of wanting her so much that I'd run her away from me." He smiled as he thought about Fidelia. "But I found I have more freedom with her love. And there's a peace that comes from knowing she loves me as I do her."

"There is no such sentiment between Davina and me," Slims murmured.

"You're a fool if you can't see it," Bears said, gripping the man's arm. "Don't let fear steal this chance from you." He looked into Slims's gaze, lit by the faint rays of the moon. "Few men have the chance to love again, and you do." He squeezed Slims's shoulder and slipped inside.

Slims stood outside, berating himself for the terror he felt. Since he was a boy and had grown into a man, he had been taught to be strong and reliable and to never show any vulnerability. He feared Davina could be his greatest weakness.

He yearned for the certainty he'd had when he had asked for her hand not even an hour ago. *Love.* Oh, how that word terrified him. He had thought he could marry Davina, enjoy her wit and her presence in his life, but keep the essential part of himself separate from her. *What a fool*, he berated himself. Every moment in her presence, every laugh he heard, every smile that had lit his day, had pulled him deeper under her spell, and he knew no day would ever be wonderful if she weren't in it. He clung to the rail as panic set in, staring up at the night's sky, praying for her to care for him with an equal fervor.

CHAPTER 6

D avina stood in the hallway, leading into the living room, crammed full with all her newfound family and friends, her hands fisted in the skirt of the finest dress she had brought from Scotland. The light-blue cotton dress with buttons down the front had a scalloped neckline and was more suited for spring or summer. However, she knew she wouldn't be cold inside the full house with the stoves pumping out heat. Her anticipation for her wedding night warmed her from the inside too. She flushed and firmed her shoulders, intent on focusing on the ceremony.

"Are ye sure, Davina?" Ewan asked. as he stood beside her.

She gripped his arm and nodded. "Aye," she whispered, although she couldn't completely mask the panic in her voice. "I pray I am not mistaken, but I trust he's a good man."

Ewan squeezed her hand. "Oh, he's a good man. An' he kens he'll have hell to pay from all of us if he ever mistreats ye." He smiled fondly at her, as he saw her eyes fill with tears at his declaration. "Ye ken ye're one of us now. We protect those we love."

"Thank ye, Ewan," she whispered, tugging on his arm to

prevent him from stepping into the doorway, signaling that the ceremony was to begin. When he stared at her in confusion, she whispered, "Thank ye for rescuing my trunk an' for acceptin' me. Ye could have rejected me because I'm no' a MacKinnon."

He shook his head, as though that were a foreign concept. "Ye ken 'tis no' our way." He leaned forward and whispered, "Ye've made yer man wait long enough with the miserable preacher for company. Save him." When she laughed, he motioned for her to follow him into the doorway.

Davina continued to chuckle, and she smiled brilliantly when she gazed down the makeshift aisle to stare at Slims, standing in his rumpled clothes. No one in town was large enough to lend him a new suit for his wedding day. She focused on the quiet promise in his gaze, the joy that lit his eyes to a warm caramel color, feeling as though she too were warmed by his deep emotions.

The preacher cleared his throat and opened his Bible. Harold stood beside the man, thumping him on his back once, before Harold stepped aside. Cruikshanks glared at Harold and then attempted to paste on a more welcoming expression, although it merely made him look gaseous.

Ignoring Pastor Cruikshanks, Davina approached Slims, her smile hopeful and her gaze filled with girlish dreams she had thought lost to her. However, the evening wedding in a new land with a new family around her acted as a kindling to feed her dreams. Standing before Slims, she gazed at him, as though this wedding had been planned for months, and finally she was allowed to fulfill her heart's desire.

He reached forward and gripped her hands as the pastor began to speak. Rather than focus on the pastor's words, she stared deeply into Slims's eyes, praying the promises she saw within were not a mirage. That they would not disappear as easily as mist at dawn's rays.

When Slims squeezed her hands, she turned to face the pastor, who stared at her with mild concern. "Aye?" she breathed.

"Will you say your vows or is this truly a farcical marriage?"

"Cruiks!" Harold snapped.

"I'll say my vows," Davina said in a low, sweet voice. "I merely found starin' in my husband's eyes more interestin' than anythin' ye had to say."

Snickers and stifled laughter rippled through the room as Pastor Cruikshanks flushed as red as a ripe tomato. "Well, I've never heard such insolence at the wedding altar before. And he's not your husband yet! You should remain hopeful that I finish this mockery of a wedding. I should have known better than to expect a MacKinnon to know how to show respect ..."

"Pastor, the vows," Slims said in a low, forceful voice.

Pastor Cruikshanks took a deep breath and let it out in a huff, before reciting the vows for Davina to repeat. Once she had said hers, Slims said his, slipping a ring onto her finger.

"By the power vested in me, although I sincerely doubt this is a wise decision, and I fear you will soon be drowning in misery, I pronounce you husband and wife!"

Davina ignored the pastor and stared expectantly at her husband, gasping when he gave her a short passionate kiss. She backed away from Slims at the roar of approval from the MacKinnons and friends, blushing as she stood beside her husband.

Soon everyone had approached them to congratulate them, and the pastor had been relegated to the kitchen, a glass of whiskey in one hand and a huge slab of Annabelle's cake in another to calm his nerves. "Dinna worry about the man," Ewan said. "We'll have him so addled by the time he returns home to his missus that he'll tell the entire town about the beautiful weddin'. He'll make the townsfolk jealous to have missed another MacKinnon ceremony."

"Ye're a rascal, are ye no'?" Davina said with affection in her voice. Already Ewan was one of her favorite people.

"Aye, an' I'm proud of it. If there's any justice in the world, wee Aileana will be one too."

Davina laughed and accepted hugs from Leticia, Jessamine, and Helen. Davina lingered to speak with Helen. "Yer husband does no' seem pleased about the marriage." She glanced in the direction of Warren Clark, the town's lawyer, who stood to one side of the celebrating MacKinnons with a forbidding expression.

"Don't worry about him. He has a case that's tying him in knots. He'll have a glass of whiskey and eat a piece of delicious cake, and then he'll relax."

Soon Davina and Slims had been pulled into the kitchen to partake of the wedding cake Annabelle had made, and any concern Davina had had about the pastor or Warren was eclipsed by the joy of the moment. She stared around at everyone delighted for her, marveling at her change in fate. All, even Warren Clark, were laughing, joking, and in good cheer. For an instant, she recalled her first wedding celebration. A bleak affair with little joy and an abundance of pretentious posturing by both families. This festive occasion seemed like a dream.

She stood beside Slims, as Cailean called for everyone to quiet.

After his third try, the raucous group fell silent. "I should ken better than to wait until after whiskey an' cake to speak," he said, as everyone chuckled. His accent had subtly reappeared with the whiskey and his deep emotions. He stared at Davina with a warm fondness, before gazing at Slims with friendship. "I know you do not ken us well, but I always give a blessin' for the important events, and I'd like to bestow one on you now."

Davina heard Slims's breath catch, and she nodded. "Aye," she whispered.

"Davina, never doubt the joy your arrival has brought the family. Never doubt our devotion to ye." He smiled as he saw the tears in her eyes. "Slims, ye've been a good, honorable friend to all, and we are entrusting our beloved cousin to you."

Davina felt Slims stiffen beside her, before his arm wrapped around her waist, holding her close to his side.

Cailean raised his glass of whiskey. "May you always find peace in the moments you spend together. May kindness flavor every argument. May prosperity be a ready companion and want a distant acquaintance. And may your home, and hearts, always be filled with love."

Sniffling, Davina leaned into Slims's side, whispering her thanks to her cousin, as everyone raised a glass to the newly-weds, cheering for them. She marveled that such a toast, such a moment, was ever meant for her.

$\sim$

Hours later, Davina walked into the small cabin behind the livery and near Cailean's house, casting a furtive glance over her shoulder to ensure her husband followed her. *My husband*, she thought and shook her head. Any wonder faded at the glowering sober man who trudged behind her. She looked forward, blindly standing in the middle of the cabin as she realized any exhibition of joy or eagerness on his part had been fabricated for the MacKinnons' benefit. Now that they were alone together, he failed to smile. He would not look at her. He refused to carry her over the threshold of the cabin. She had clung to hope that this marriage would be different. That, this time, she alone would be enough. *I'm the fool.*

She jolted when the door closed with a *thud* and the latch sounded, her gaze focusing on the intimate space. In one corner was a large bed with a patchwork quilt covering it. She recognized it as Sorcha's handiwork. In the other corner was a small kitchen area, and a stove had been lit to heat the room. A blanket instead of a door covered a doorway in the wall, and she walked to it, peering through it to see a small bed inside. With another glance over her shoulder, she saw Slims with his back to her, staring out the window.

With a huff, she slipped into the small room, intent on sleeping alone in the small bed that night. "If he thinks I'm sleeping with him tonight, he's an *eejit*," she muttered, clinging to her righteous anger, rather than focusing on the pain that would overwhelm her, if she gave it free rein. Thankfully the buttons of her dress were on the front, and she easily slipped them free. She set it at the foot of the bed, as there was little room for a chair in the small room. She eased off her corset and crawled under the blankets, shivering at the cool sheets. Belatedly she realized the warmth of the stove in the front room would not reach her back here. However, she was determined not to gift him with anything more tonight.

Curling onto her side, she pulled the blankets over her head and finally allowed the silent tears to course down her cheeks. She buried her face in her pillow to silence her sobs, and she released her pent-up anguish. Soon she slipped into a restless sleep, dreaming of a magical wedding night, where she slept in her husband's arms, feeling cherished and adored.

~

S lims stood in what had been Bears's small cabin, staring out the window. His mind was filled with visions of the wedding ceremony. He battled a groan as he recalled his first view of Davina, beautiful in a light-blue dress with her hair pulled back in a soft bun. His fingers had itched to free her silky blond hair from its pins and to watch the beautiful mass cascade down her back. He fought a chuckle as he recalled the dyspeptic pastor, red-faced, spitting out the words of the ceremony.

Only the presence of Harold Tompkins had induced Pastor Cruikshanks to finish the ceremony and to choke out a blessing at the end. Slims sighed as he thought of the softest, most chaste kiss of his life. Closing his eyes, he remembered the silky touch of her lips against his and his battle not to deepen it.

"Fool," he muttered to himself. He turned to look for Davina, belatedly realizing he didn't hear her moving around the small space. He had thought she'd bustle around the kitchen or act as though she had a chore to do before they would go to bed. Frowning, he didn't see her. Terror filled him at the thought that she had slipped out into the winter's night, already dissatisfied at having married him. Before racing outside and sounding an alarm, he poked his head into the spare room Ewan had constructed on the back of the cabin for Bears's daughter, Mildred.

Slims froze when he saw her, curled on her side, asleep. Her chest rose and fell in an even cadence, and he shook his head in disbelief. "Why wouldn't you sleep with me, Dav?" he whispered.

He stood for long minutes, watching her sleep, and then he spun out of the room to pace the small front room. Eventually he decided to ready for bed. After he had shucked his pants and shirt, but kept on his underclothes, he pulled down the blankets and the top sheet on the big bed. On tiptoes, he crept into the back room and eased her into his arms. When she wrapped her arms around his neck, whispering, "Simon," a fraction of the anger and the hurt he felt eased.

"Come, love. Time for bed," he whispered, kissing her head.

He settled her in the larger bed and climbed in after her, wrapping an arm around her waist as he pulled her against him. The blankets were tucked around them, and the fire was strong enough to keep them warm for a few hours. He fell asleep, at peace with her in his arms.

Davina woke, grumbling her protest as the arm around her waist slipped free and the warmth along her back eased from the bed. "No," she murmured, her hands reaching out and grasping at air. "No," she cried, tears coursing down her cheeks as she pushed her face into the pillow. It had all been a dream. Laying in Slims's arms, feeling cherished and adored by him, feeling wanted for the first time in so long. Nothing more than a fantasy. Why could nothing in her life ever measure up to the dreams she created while she slept?

She squealed when the bed sagged beside her, and a large body rested beside her again. Rolling over, she bashed into his chest. "What?" she gasped. "Ye're real?"

Chuckling, Slims swiped at her tears and then at tendrils of her hair that had escaped from the hasty braid she had tied when she went to bed. "Of course I am. What did you think?" he whispered, his brown eyes filled with concern, as he seemed to understand she was on the verge of panic. "*Shh,* Davina, I'm here. You're safe."

She pushed forward, wrapping her arms and legs around

him. "I thought ye were a dream," she whispered into his neck. "Sent to torment me but never to be real."

"No, my little one, no," he murmured, kissing her head. "I'm very real. A man of flesh and bone, who will make mistakes and disappoint you." He paused as he felt her calming in his arms. "I upset you last night because you went to bed in the other room."

She let out a huff of disgust as she looked up at him, now fully awake. "Of course I did. Ye looked like a man bein' led to the gallows." She nodded as he gaped at her. "Any self-respectin' woman would be angry. Especially when it's her weddin' night!"

"I couldn't have looked like that," he said, as he cupped her cheek. He gripped her shoulders to keep her in place when she huffed out a breath and moved to turn away from him. "Look at me. Listen to me," he said in a deep, melodious voice.

She stilled as she stared deeply into his gaze, lit by the faint light of the fire.

"I won't lie, Dav. I won't." He took a deep breath and expelled it. "I was terrified but not because I'd married you. Because I'd married at all." He waited a moment, as though hoping to see a softening in her expression, but all he saw was wariness and uncertainty. "I'd sworn never to marry, and, within weeks of meeting you, I was standing in front of a preacher, vowing to protect you, honor you, forever. I fear that you'll be gravely disappointed in your choice of me and that I'll fail you." He closed his eyes a moment.

"Do ye think I dinna feel the same?" she asked, as she ran her fingers over his whiskers.

His eyes flew open, as he gazed at her again. "I'll never be disappointed in you." He kissed her fingers as they neared his lips. "And you'll never fail." He watched her with fervent intensity, as her eyes shone with unshed tears at his avowal.

She marshaled her courage at his words. "Why would ye no' carry me over the threshold? Why would ye no' touch me once we left Cailean's house?"

His hand that had drifted to her hip tightened its hold on her there. "I wanted you so much, Davina," he breathed. "I didn't want you to see that side of me." She frowned, and he dropped his hands away. "I'm sorry. I've offended you. I should never have forced you to sleep beside me. It was selfish ..."

She covered his mouth with her soft hands, her eyes beseeching him to quiet. "Hush, Simon," she whispered. She took a deep breath and flushed, her gaze never wavering from his. "I fear I very much want to see that side of ye. I want to ken ye have a madness for me that I do for ye." Her eyes filled. "The thought that ye did no', that I was the only one mad with the need to touch ye ..." She shook her head as tears leaked down her cheeks. "I could no' bear such a marriage again."

"You aren't, Dav." He sighed, resting his forehead against hers. "You aren't." He sat back a few inches. "There's something I very much want to do, something only a husband should do, but I don't want to offend you."

Her eyes sparkled with humor and mischief. "Aye? An' what's that?"

His large hands rose to trace over her head. "I very much want to see your hair unbound and in my hands. Let me free it."

She closed her eyes with pleasure at the soft touch of his hands on her head, gently massaging her scalp. "Oh, aye, husband," she gasped, as his fingers loosened the braid and moved through the silky strands. She sat, with an expression of supreme pleasure as he played with her hair, sighing with delight as he eased her onto her side so he could loosen her braid.

"How beautiful," he murmured. "I never thought to be the lucky one to see it free again. That day it fell loose, that first day in Fred's living room, I thought my heart would stop at the beauty of it," he rasped, as he leaned forward and kissed his way down her spine, his mouth following the path of his fingers.

"'Tis terribly heavy," she said. "I've thought of cuttin' it off."

He finished loosening her hair and spread it out, letting it fall though his fingers. When she had turned to him again, he looked deeply into her gaze, as though assessing her real question. "I'd want you, with or without your beautiful hair, Davina. What matters to me is the woman you are, in here." He placed a hand over her heart, frowning as he saw her eyes shimmer with tears. "You are a remarkable woman, and I'm the luckiest of men to call you my wife."

Her eyes shone with pleasure. "Kiss me," she whispered.

Tracing a finger over her cheek, he leaned forward and paused inches from her lips. "If I kiss you, I won't be able to stop. I want you too much."

A tremulous, hopeful smile bloomed. "There's no such thing as *too much*," she whispered. "Be darin', Simon."

Callused fingers scraped over her silky skin, and he breached the last few inches, "I will be. Only for you."

Slims rested with a slumbering Davina in his arms. He knew he should try to sleep, but it eluded him. Every soft breath, each quiet snuffle, or shift of her head captivated him. He feared the day this fascination faded and worried what it would mean when the ability to hold her in his arms was not a novelty. Saying a silent prayer, he hoped he never took his beautiful wife for granted. That he always gave thanks for her presence in his life and in his arms. For his life had been a long and lonely one, and he had no desire to return to such a life.

She murmured a soft word and shifted in his arms. Kissing her head, he whispered soothing words, and she calmed. He found himself praying again that she would always find solace in his embrace. That she'd never look to another for the comfort she should find with him. She moaned in his arms, and he rubbed his hand down her side. "*Shh*, Davina, you're well. You're safe."

"Simon?" she whispered.

"Yes, sweetheart," he murmured, kissing her head again. "I'm here."

She moved and then groaned with the slight movement.

He grimaced. "Forgive me," he murmured, kissing her head softly and wrapping his arms gently around her. "I was not as gentle as I should have been. I promise you'll never ache again."

She kissed his forearm and snuggled back into him. Her voice was slurred with sleep, but he could make out what she said. "Ye should apologize," she said around a large yawn. When he froze at her words, she giggled. She squirmed until she faced him, and she cupped his face, the touch of the soft skin of her palms making him groan with pleasure. "Ye've made me crave ye." She arched up and kissed him. "Never before have I felt such passion." She kissed him again and smiled, as he stared at her in wonder. "Or such pleasure." Another long kiss. "And now ye say ye'll no' love me like that again?" She stared at him with hurt in her gaze. "Whyever no'? Did ye no' feel—" She bit her lip as insecurity and embarrassment filled her gaze.

"Davina," he breathed. "I worried I hurt you."

She shook her head. "Look at me," she urged. "Do I look like I'm tremblin' in fear at the sight of ye?" Her smile bloomed. "I might be tremblin' because I canna wait to kiss ye again an' have ye in my arms again, but no' because I fear ye." Her smile dimmed. "That makes me wanton, no? A respectable woman should no' speak in such a way."

He groaned in disagreement, kissing her passionately until they were both breathless. "My woman, *my wife*, tells me what she likes and doesn't like. And, if she finds pleasure in my touch," he said in a low, deep voice as he brushed away long tendrils of her hair, "then I will have to discover ways of giving her more and more pleasure every day."

"Oh, yes, please," Davina breathed as she arched up to his touch. "Ye dinna ken how long I've waited ..." She gasped as he kissed her collarbone.

He kissed his way up her neck and murmured, "I have an idea, darlin'." He met her yearning-filled gaze. "Let me love you again."

"Yes," she breathed.

Simon said another prayer, that her passionate honesty would never abate. For he didn't know what he would do without it now that he had experienced it.

The following morning, bright light streamed in through cracks in the curtain, creating a kaleidoscope pattern on the floor and bed. Davina snuggled into Slims's side, intent on remaining in bed for as long as possible.

"Are you awake, darlin'?" he murmured, his work-roughened hands caressing the silky skin of her shoulders and back.

"Aye, although I dinna want to be. I want to stay here forever," she breathed, as she pressed into his chest. She smiled as she heard the rumble of his laughter against her ear.

"I fear I'll need sustenance at some point, darlin'." He kissed the top of her head. "And we should return to the ranch today."

Davina moaned in protest, wrapping her arms and legs around Slims. "Nae."

"Don't you want to see your cousin?" he asked. He eased her away, brushing at her hair, tangled in knots as it framed her face. "Dav?"

"I want time with just ye, Simon." She ducked her head. "I ken I'm selfish, but I want time to talk with ye and to sit in silence if we want. Time without interruptions."

Sighing, he brushed featherlight strokes over her cheek. "As do I," he murmured. "But I'm foreman of an important ranch. I need to be there, Dav." When she flushed and seemed to deflate in front of him, he cupped her cheek to tilt her face up to meet his gaze. "My work and my duty to Frederick and the men will never be more important than you, Davina. You are my wife, and you will always come first." He paused. "But I also must provide a good living for us, as well as be true to myself. And part of that is doing my job well."

She bit her lip, her brown eyes filled with adoration as she gazed at him. "I have faith in ye, Simon. I ken how the men respect ye and how Frederick relies on ye." She shrugged. "I had hoped for more than one night with ye."

A smile burst forth as his thumb rubbed her lips. "Oh, we'll have more than one night, my darlin'. We'll have every night to come."

She flushed and fell forward to again rest in his strong arms. "I ... I must tell ye somethin'." She paused as her fingers played in his short chest hairs. "I'm a bit of an heiress." When he tensed, she turned her head, so she could meet his gaze. "When I left Scotland, I sewed coins and jewels into the hem of my petticoats and cape."

He gaped at her, before bursting out laughing. "Oh, you

are brilliant." After awaiting a long moment to see if she would say anything more, he said, "When we next come to town together, we can visit the bank and place them in a safe there, if you like."

She let out a deep breath. "Ye are no' angry at me?" At his quizzical expression, she whispered, "For no' tellin' ye afore? I let ye marry me, thinkin' I was a poor woman." She shrieked as Slims rolled them so he hovered over her, his eyes lit with a passionate fervency.

"If you were as poor as that destitute Mrs. Jameson, I would have wanted you, Davina," he breathed. "You are what I desire. Not any jewels or coin you might have brought with you from Scotland. *You.*"

A tear trickled free, as she ran her fingers through his hair and gripped his shoulder. "'Twill take me time to understand what ye mean."

He smiled. "Take as long as you need, darlin'. We have the rest of our lives."

~

Later that morning, Davina opened the front door to the bakery and halted as the scents of freshly baked bread, cookies, and cakes wafted over her. She inhaled and then sighed with the deepest pleasure. "Heaven," she breathed.

Chuckling, Slims agreed. "Yes, it's my favorite place to visit in town. Besides the café."

She looked over her shoulder, her gaze filled with appreciation as she beheld her handsome husband. "Ye're very loyal, are ye no'?"

He shrugged and ushered her inside.

Davina moved around the space, staring at the shelves filled with Fidelia's fine lace and Sorcha's beautiful wool to be sold. Davina then moved to the glass-fronted case with the pastries and breads. "'Tis a wee bit of paradise."

Jane entered and smiled. "Davina!" she exclaimed, running around the case to pull her into a hug. "Oh, I'm so excited for you and Slims." Her broad smile took in both of them. "I didn't have an opportunity to congratulate you last night."

"'Twas a bit chaotic," Davina said, "but lovely."

"Oh, it was a beautiful ceremony. It reminded me of mine, although Warren presided over my wedding. And we had a little less time to prepare." She slipped her arm through Davina's and pulled her along with her. "Come to the back. You can visit with everyone while we work."

Davina walked beside Jane, casting a glance over her shoulder to ensure Slims followed. When Davina entered the kitchen, she paused to see Fidelia sitting in a rocking chair in a corner with Jack at her breast, Jessamine pacing as she told a story, Annabelle laughing at whatever Jessamine had said, and Leena watching it all, wide-eyed.

"Davina!" Annabelle proclaimed. "Oh, I feared we wouldn't see you again before you left to return to the ranch."

Davina was enfolded in embraces, each woman giving her a searching look before smiling with satisfaction. Flushing, Davina stammered, "I insisted I must see the bakery afore we left. An' I thought we could bring back a little somethin' for Sorcha, Frederick, an' the men."

"Of course," Annabelle said, swiping her hands on her apron and then staring at horror at Davina's clothes. "I've covered you in flour."

"'Tis no bother," Davina said with a laugh. She reached behind her for Slims's hand, relaxing subtly when his hand was in hers. "Ye have a beautiful bakery."

Annabelle smiled her thanks. "It's a good business, and we

have fun working here and gossiping our time away. A small room is through there that functions as a nursery. Little Aileana's having a rest right now, and Skye insisted on watching over her." She smiled at Davina. "And the extra income is always welcome."

The bell over the front door jingled, and Jane scurried to the front, where her friendly voice could be heard as she served a patron.

"I've been fortunate to have this bakery and such fine friends and family to run it with." Annabelle yawned. "Now I'd suggest bread, cookies, and one of our cakes." She looked at Slims. "What do you think?"

"If possible, could we bring two cakes?" He smiled as the women laughed at his request.

Soon their order was packed up in a crate, and Davina faced her cousins and friends. "I dinna want to say goodbye."

"It's not forever," Jessamine said, as she pulled her into a tight embrace. "It's just for now. We'll see you again soon."

Fidelia squeezed her hand. "You'll have so many adventures on the ranch that you'll forget about missing us."

Davina battled tears and shook her head. "I ken I'll have adventures, but I'll still miss ye."

She hugged Annabelle and then preceded Slims out the door. When they were outside, she let out a stuttering breath. "Forgive me," she whispered, as she looked at her feet.

Holding the box of goodies in one arm, he used his free hand to tip up her chin so she would meet his gaze. "What is there to forgive?" he murmured. "The fact you like, perhaps even love, your family? Why is that something to be ashamed of?"

"I'm no' ashamed." She sniffled and shrugged. "I'm embarrassed."

He smiled tenderly at her. "I think, for too long, you've learned to hide your emotions and to bottle them up. Let 'em loose, Davina. I can handle them. And you." He waited as he saw her eyes widen in surprise. "I'd far rather know how you feel than have to guess. I'm certain I'd always guess wrong."

"I should no' burden another with my emotions," she protested.

"Hogwash," he snapped. His finger traced her cheek. "Your emotions, how you feel, will never be a burden to me, Dav. Remember that."

She stared at him in wonder, before nodding. "Ye do no' feel as though I'm betrayin' ye because I'm sad to leave my family?"

"Hell no," he said with a tender smile. "I'd think you a fool if you could leave all this and be unaffected."

She stepped forward, into his embrace. "Thank ye, Simon," she whispered. "I will miss them, but I'm ready to go home."

~

Slims knew he was being fanciful. He knew his heightened awareness of the world around him came from his appreciation for the woman beside him and for the pleasure he had felt in her arms the previous night. Even so, he marveled at the valley blanketed in fresh snow and the drifts piled high from the fierce winds. The trees in the distance appeared as though covered in powdered sugar, their brilliant green branches dulled by a fine white coating of snow. It felt as though he were seeing the valley for the first time.

He recalled their conversation outside the bakery this morning and was filled with a sense of triumph. At the unfettered joy he had felt at her referring to the ranch, and thus her life with him, as *home*. Home. He had never felt more grateful for a simple word in his entire life.

He glanced down at Davina, when she shivered and moved closer to Slims as they passed by the turnoff to the small cabin. He half wished they could return to it and escape returning to the ranch. The other half of him never wanted to return there, for he feared any harm ever befalling his Davina. He knew they had been extremely fortunate that night.

When he felt her stiffen beside him, Slims reached out his hand, grasping hers for a moment, before he had to keep ahold of the reins. "There's no need to be tense, Dav," he murmured. "No one will be upset we married." He smiled at her and then winced. "Except Sorcha. She'll be irate she missed another wedding. She loves weddings."

Davina wrapped her arm through his, tugging the blanket over them as much as possible, as she sat cuddled up beside him on the sleigh. "I hate denyin' her the chance to see us wed, but I canna say I'm sad the preacher wed us. He was none pleased about it, but it should help with the gossipin' townsfolk."

Slims shook his head, as he steered the sleigh toward the lane leading to the ranch. "Aye," he murmured, leaning to the side to kiss her head. "I'll have to ask Frederick what a good gift for his grandparents would be. Harold deserves something special for cornering that man into marryin' us."

She giggled and waved at Shorty, as he raced from the barn to meet them as the sleigh bells jingled, heralding their arrival. "Shorty, 'tis good to see ye!"

Shorty scratched at his head, his astute gaze taking in the cozy way Davina sat beside Slims. "Seems you have a tale or two to tell after your trip to town. Did you make it in before the storm?"

Slims hopped down and then helped Davina out. "No. Got stuck in one of the old cabins. Had to hole up for the night." Shorty watched him with a fierce intensity in his gaze.

"Caused some ruckus in town." Unable to help it, he beamed at his friend. "Davina and I married last night."

Shorty's eyes bulged, and he belatedly sputtered out a stuttering, "Congratulations." He eyed Slims as though he were about to become mired in the pigpen but then shook his head, muttering, "Some things can keep another day." In a louder voice, he said, "I'll see to the horses and to the unloading of the supplies with Dix and Dalton. You should enjoy a short ... honeymoon." Again his voice faltered, and he shook his head at his friend.

"Thanks, Short," Slims said, nudging Davina away from the sleigh and toward a cabin on the opposite side of the driveway, away from the big house. When she stumbled in the snow, he swung her into his arms, laughing as she shrieked.

He pushed open the door and carried her inside. "Welcome to our home," he murmured, looking around the small, slightly dusty space. "If I'd known we were to marry, I would have had the men clean it up." He set her on her feet, watching her intently as she glanced around the small space. A kitchen and a table were to one side with a small stove that would heat the room, with a bed pressed into a corner. In the free space were a rocking chair and a gentleman's high-backed chair. "I know it's not much ..."

She stood on her toes and pressed her hands over his lips. "Nae, ye dinna ken what I'm thinkin'." Her luminous smile made his breath catch. "I woke this mornin', wishin' we could have a cozy home like the one we slept in last night. An' now we do." She looked around with wonder. "'Tis more than I could have hoped for."

"Davina," he breathed, tugging her into his arms.

"An' then, to have ye carry me over the threshold." She sighed. "Thank ye, Simon. I was distraught last night that ye would no'."

He shook his head in confusion. "Why would I? That wasn't our home. This is."

Her smile softened. "Aye. *Home.*" Linking her hand with his, she stilled at the knock on the door.

Slims released his hold on her, answering the door to see Dalton, Dixon, and Shorty outside. Shorty carried food, while Dalton and Dixon hefted in armfuls of wood. "Thank you," Slims said.

"Short told us the news," Dixon said, yelping when Dalton hit him on his arm with a piece of wood as he was about to say something more. "Congratulations."

Slims watched the interplay between the men but decided it wasn't something he cared to worry about tonight. Tomorrow would bring her problems soon enough. For now, he wanted to spend more time with Davina and to learn as much about her as he could.

"Thank ye, Mr. Dixon," Davina said. She giggled as each man kissed her on her cheek, before traipsing out the door.

Slims sighed as he shut and latched the door. He moved to the stove to build a fire to heat their small home. "They'll be as loyal to you as they are to me," he said.

She watched him in confusion, as she settled in the rocking chair. "Why? They dinna ken me as they do ye. I've done little to earn their loyalty, except cook them meals. There is no reason for them to be loyal to me."

Slims waited for the kindling to catch, the light from the flames playing over his face. "You're my wife. Thus they will respect you as they do me."

Shaking her head, she smiled. "I dinna ken a thing about runnin' a ranch. I hope they dinna expect me to give them orders on the proper way to work with the beasts ye have wanderin' this land."

He chuckled. "They're cattle, not some mythical creatures, and I'm afraid you'll soon know more than you want to about the running of a ranch." He watched her as she gazed at him with adoration and hope. "I fear this will be an isolating life for you, Davina."

She reached forward, her fingers tracing the strong lines of his jaw and scraping through his whiskers. "Nae, never. I have a cousin with bairns here an' more family than I could have imagined in town. I may not ken much about ranch life, but I'm certain there will always be work for me to do." She bit her lip. "An' I'll have ye, aye?"

He smiled, moving to her and falling onto his knees before her. He ran a hand over her braided hair and then down her arm. "Aye, always."

~

Davina snuggled into Slims's arms, ignoring the small voice in her head that warned her that she was adapting too readily to being in another man's arms. Where had her desire to live as an independent woman gone? She kissed his shoulder and pushed aside that thought as she sighed with contentment.

"Are you well, darlin'?"

She shivered at his tender question and tone, pressing tighter against him. "Aye," she whispered, suddenly battling a severe shyness. She rested her head on his shoulder, wanting to hide her gaze from his.

"What's this?" he asked, tilting her head up to him. "Come, Davina. There's no need for shyness now. Not after bouts of lovemakin'." He chuckled as her body blushed pink at his words. He ran a soft hand over her back and up again. "Do you … Would you prefer I found another place to sleep tonight?"

"Nae!" she gasped, her hands clawing into his shoulders

to keep him in place. She smiled up at him as he chuckled and nodded.

"Good," he said. "But I don't want you to feel uneasy due to my presence."

She dropped her head, her eyes closed, as though saying a silent prayer. "I never thought to find comfort laying in a man's arms again." She opened her eyes to meet his ardent gaze. "I believed such joy was to forever be denied me."

He tugged her even tighter into his embrace, smattering kisses over her head, cheeks, and neck. "You are a woman meant to be treasured, adored, and well loved. I still can't believe I'm the man fortunate enough to hold you like this."

She kissed him but broke off the kiss as a torrent of tears poured out with such speed that he couldn't brush them away with his fingers. They broke over his hands, as though a river overflowing a dam, dripping off her chin. She tried to turn away from him to hide her embarrassing display of emotions, but he only held her close as her tears wet his chest.

"No, Davina, no, love," he murmured, as he held her close, rocking her side to side as she sobbed. "*Shh*, my darlin', you are safe. No one will hurt you here. I promise on all I am as a man." He continued to hold her and to soothe her with soft words until her breaths came out in staccato bursts.

"Forgive me," she said in a creaky voice. "How mortifyin'."

He shook his head, cupping her cheeks in his palms to prevent her from turning away from him. "No, my darlin', not at all. What you just shared with me was as truthful as our lovemakin'. And as great a gift. Thank you." He kissed her forehead, sighing with a deep sense of peace. "Thank you for trusting me with your pain."

She shook her head, her shoulders rising and falling slightly. "I dinna ken why, but I do."

His brown eyes shone with a fierce pleasure at her words.

127

"Please be honest with me, Davina. Tell me what it was like with your husband. What did he do to smother the fire that burns so brightly inside you?"

Another tear formed, finally freeing and rolling down her cheek. "He was no' a bad man, aye? Never hit me." She shuddered at the thought. "I kent enough women who suffered that plight. Husband gone with drink, an' he claims he dinna ken what he was doin'." She shook her head. "Nae, I thought myself fortunate because Ian only wanted a clean house and supper on the table."

She looked at her hands, which had unconsciously risen to grip Slims's shoulders, as though taking strength from him. With a sigh, she continued. "I quickly learned there are other ways to inflict punishment. Words are as strong a weapon as a fist, aye?"

He nodded, his hold on her gentle.

"I was deemed a tease an' a flirt because I danced with a man at the harvest dance. I was also vain and conceited because I wouldna cut my hair." Her voice emerged in stuttering breaths. "I was worthless as a woman because I could not bear bairns who would live outside my womb." She ducked her head. "I was a failure, a pathetic excuse for a woman," she whispered.

"Lies," Slims rasped. "All lies." He waited for her to look at him, but she kept her head lowered. After long minutes, she finally met his gaze. "You are magnificent and brave and the most worthy woman I have ever met. I'd kill anyone who dared to harm you or to speak such vile words to you," he vowed.

"What if I can't give you a child, Slims?" Her eyes glowed with the agony of her fear. "I ken ye said ye dinna care, but all men want a son. Ye'll come to think of me as Ian did."

He growled, clasping her head and leaning forward so their foreheads touched. They both breathed fast, sharing the same air. "Never compare me to that worthless excuse for a man. He had heaven in his arms and didn't have the sense to know it." He eased away, his thumbs caressing under her eyes, as though searching for errant tears. "I do not lie to you, Davina, and I never will. That is a vow I make to you."

He waited for her to nod. "If we have a baby, for however long he or she lives, I will cherish him or her." He cleared his throat, as though it were constricted from a deep emotion. "I will not lie and say the thought of a bairn with you doesn't fill me with joy. And terror." He smiled at her tenderly. "And I will mourn if he or she is not with us for longer than a few months." His gaze bore into hers with a fierce determination. "But I would never take out my pain on you. And I would never allow you to mourn alone and to bear the brunt of that suffering to ease my own. I want to share everything, the good and the bad with you, Davina. That is what I dream of for our marriage."

"Slims," she whispered. "Be patient with me." She turned her face into his soft caress. "I want the same, but I canna give up my fears so easily."

"I will dream, every day, that the pleasure of your present outweighs the pain of your past," he breathed as he arched down to kiss her.

"Slims?" she whispered, hours later, when she knew she should be asleep. The soft rhythm of his breathing continued unabated, and she knew he was asleep. However, he raised a hand to brush at her long hair shining in the faint light like a beacon.

"Yes, my darling?" he asked, his breathing unchanged and eyes closed.

"How many others have ye … cared for as ye care for me?" She winced as she felt him freeze beneath her.

"None," he breathed, heaving out a sigh. His gaze met hers, and he stared at her with blatant curiosity.

"What about the woman from your youth?" she whispered, biting her lip as his gaze shone with the remnants of that betrayal.

"I thank God every day you're nothing like her," he whispered. "She was hell-bent on bringing about my destruction and ruining everything I held dear. You, you are the opposite."

Davina blushed with his praise.

"I've not been a monk, Davina."

She froze at those words, flushed, and nodded. "Of course not. I'm no' a fool. I ken what men are."

"What men are?" he asked with a tilt of his head. "Not all men will prove a disappointment." He lowered his voice to a near whisper, but it was all the more potent for its low volume. "I've not visited the Boudoir. Not once." He waited for her to meet his gaze again. When she did, he gave a grunt of approval. "The last woman who interested me, well, she found another man."

"When was that?" Davina traced circles on his chest and held her breath.

"Not too long ago." He chuckled. "But then time's relative when you're as old as I am and livin' on a ranch with few prospects."

He moved so she was underneath him, earning a squeal of delight in surprise, and held her hands in his. His gaze roved over her, filled with satisfaction and a seemingly endless well of desire. "How I want you, lass," he murmured, having picked up that word from Sorcha and her family. He paused as he detected something in her gaze. "And it's not just the physical. I want to know what you think. What you dream

130

about. What interests you." He paused, flushing as she stared at him in wonder but remained silent. "Forgive me. I know few desire such a marriage."

He released her arms and flopped onto his back, letting out a huff of frustration as he stared at the ceiling, while the wood crackled in the stove.

"Nae!" she gasped, following him until she sprawled on his chest. "Ye misunderstand. I never thought to have a marriage like ye describe." She swallowed as she bravely met his guarded gaze. "I never dreamed a man could want such a marriage with me."

He let out a harsh breath, tugging her up his body until he could kiss her. She sat with her legs around his waist and her arms propped on his shoulder, holding him close as the kiss deepened. His hands twisted in her hair, while his tongue tangled with hers. Breaking the kiss, he gasped out, "Only a fool wouldn't want such a marriage with you, Dav. You're every man's dream, come to life."

Davina bit her lip, fighting her instinctual need to protect herself and thus deny what he said. Instead she smiled shyly and batted her eyes at him. "Aye, I am."

He laughed, easing her to settle down onto his chest. "There," he whispered. "You'll accustom yourself to such praise, and I'll have to worry about giving you a big ego," he teased.

"Only with you, Simon," she breathed.

"Aye, my darlin', only with me."

CHAPTER 7

Davina entered the big ranch house the following day around midmorning, listening for the sounds of her cousin. Although Davina wished she could remain outside, now that it was a brilliantly bright day, it remained too cold to linger for long outdoors. Memories from the previous nights she had spent with Slims flitted through her mind, and she couldn't help a contented sigh as she looked to join her cousin and to tell her all about her adventures in town. When Davina heard Sorcha singing softly in the back room, she moved in that direction to join her, walking on silent feet so as not to awaken the babes.

She paused at the doorway, listening to the mournful song about a woman's lost love and her endless search to regain the love forever out of her reach. Shivering, Davina focused on her cousin. Rather than contentment, it appeared that Sorcha was agitated and distraught. "Hello, Sorcha," she whispered, after seeing the bairns asleep in the corner of the room.

"Davina," Sorcha said, her tormented gaze meeting hers.

"'Tis good to see ye at last." She flushed and lowered her gaze, under the pretense of focusing on her spinning wool. However, Davina had the sense Sorcha did not want to meet Davina's gaze.

"Are ye well? Did somethin' happen to the bairns while I was away?" Davina asked in a rush.

"Nae, dinna fash yerself," Sorcha murmured. "All is well." She grimaced. "As well as it can be." Her light-blue eyes shone with concern. "I was told ye married."

Davina nodded, unable to hide her overjoyed grin from her cousin. When Sorcha continued to stare at her dispassionately, Davina's smile faded, and she moved into the room to sit near her cousin. "Aye. I'm sorry if that upsets ye."

Sorcha closed her eyes and shook her head. "Of course it doesna. Slims is a good man. I'd despaired of him ever meetin' a woman he'd want to marry."

Davina stared at her in confusion. "I dinna understand. Why are ye upset? Was there somethin' in the letters Slims brought in from town that was no' to yer liking?" Davina asked. When Sorcha continued to stare at her like a storm was brewing, she sobered even further. "What is it?"

"Ye ken ye are family to me?" Sorcha asked. "Just as Slims is." She ceased spinning and set aside the wheel. "There's a complication, an' ye need to ken it."

"Tell me, Sorcha, please."

"Did Slims ever mention a woman named Charlotte Ingram?" When Davina shrugged, Sorcha reached forward and gripped her cousin's hand. "Charlotte was a cook we hired last summer. This is a large ranch, and we had a terrible winter a few years ago. As ye might ken, we almost lost our ranch. Unfortunately Frederick's neighbor went bankrupt, and Frederick cobbled together enough money to buy out that ranch. 'Tis good land. They have a homestead a few hours ride from here." She waved a hand in a vague direction away from the house.

"Why are ye tellin' me this?" Davina asked with furrowed brows. "I ken there was a fierce winter, but I dinna see why I should care the ranch is so large."

Sorcha closed her eyes and then squared her shoulders as she met her cousin's gaze. "Slims and Shorty spent the summer on their spread—the new land—moving cattle to distant grazing land. From all accounts, Charlotte drove Slims mad, and there was rumor of a love affair between them."

"No," Davina whispered, slipping her hand free of Sorcha's, as she shook her head.

"Aye," Sorcha said, with a brisk nod. "We all thought it humorous at the time. The thought of a wee slip of a woman drivin' such a big man mad. I'm sorry." She paused before blurting out, "An' now Charlotte's back, Davina. She was the cook I said disappeared in December. Do ye remember?" She paused as though weighing whether or not to impart the worst of the news. "Claims she's with child. And that Slims is the father of her babe."

"Nae!" Davina yelped, standing up quickly, slapping her hands over her mouth to still any further outburst to prevent waking the bairns. She turned one way and then the other before collapsing to the ground. "Nae," she gasped, dropping her hands to hold them to her heart, as though that alone kept it from splintering into a thousand tiny pieces. "Nae," she pleaded, as her shoulders shook.

Sorcha knelt in front of her, gripping her cousin's shoulders. "She could be lyin'. I canna lie an' say I ken her well. I dinna. I met her only a few times. Afore she went to the new land an' when she came back."

"Why would she claim something that wasna true?"

135

Davina asked, as tears seeped out and coursed down her cheek. "What could she hope to gain?"

Sorcha sighed and rubbed at her temple. "She had no idea ye were here. That ye an' Slims were in town an' that ye were to marry. I've never seen a woman more distraught than her yesterday, when Shorty came into the kitchen with the news ye'd returned and wanted time to enjoy bein' newlyweds."

Davina sat in a dazed stupor, her gaze unfocused, as she rocked forward and back. "He said he had cared for a woman recently, but she had left him for another." Her stricken gaze met Sorcha's. "Why am I always a fool?" she whispered. "Why did I ever believe in a man's promise again?" She fell forward into Sorcha's arms as insuppressible sobs burst forth.

~

Slims whistled a ribald tune as he worked mucking out a stall in the horse barn. After another passionate night with his bride, the sharing of her pasts and his truths, he felt like their relationship would only continue to grow. He had not allowed himself to feel such hope since he was a boy in Kansas, but he refused to believe this unexpected gift of Davina would be so cruelly taken away from him. For now he would focus on their everyday joys and would hope she continued to find contentment with her life with him. For he did not know what he would do if she did not.

Shorty approached him and kicked hay at him. When Slims saw him glowering at him, he frowned. "What's got you so upset? Why were you actin' odd yesterday?"

Shorty shook his head. "How could you, Slims?"

Slims looked over Shorty's shoulder and saw Frederick and Dalton standing behind his best friend, their expressions mirroring Shorty's. "What are you talking about? How could

I not?" he asked, as he set aside his pitchfork, and moved toward the men who were like brothers to him. "I married her to protect her." He smiled. "And because I'm crazy about her."

Dalton took a step forward and punched him in his shoulder, knocking him back a step because he was taken by surprise. "How could you take a bride when you'd already promised Charlotte you'd marry her?"

Slims's jaw fell open, and he gaped at his friends, before bursting into laughter. When he saw they were deadly serious, he shook his head with incredulity. "You are joking?" Looking at Shorty, he said, "Don't you remember we didn't have one kind word to say to each other last summer? That she threatened to starve me if I dared speak to her again because I was so uncivil?"

Frederick shrugged. "That reminds me of my courting Sorcha. We were always nipping at each other because we were crazy about each other."

Slims took off his gloves and slapped them on his thighs. "You cared about Sorcha. I never liked Charlotte! I've no interest in the woman! Did I seem upset when she disappeared in December? No! Good riddance!"

"And the fact she's carryin' your babe?" Dalton asked, his jaw ticking as his eyes shone with anger and challenge.

Slims froze, his eyes widening in horror. "My what?" he gasped. "No. Never. I never touched her." He held up his hands in a plea for his innocence.

A soft gasp sounded at the entrance to the barn, and a woman of middling height with reddish-blond hair entered. "How can you deny what we had?" she asked in a breathless voice, choked with tears. "How can you treat me like this?"

Slims took a step back. "Charlotte," he spat out, his voice filled with contempt. "I never treated you as anything other than you are. An opportunistic woman eager to latch on to a man of power at the ranch."

She held a hand to her belly. "You'd deny me? Deny your baby his rights?"

Slims shook his head. "You lie," he said. "And I'm married. To a woman who'd never try to deceive me." He looked at his friends and saw doubt in their gazes, although he prayed they were doubting her and not him. He looked beseechingly at Frederick. "Go into town. Fetch Helen. Have her examine Charlotte. Prove that there is no way this … this could be mine."

Charlotte threw herself at him, and he easily sidestepped her. She landed in a pile of hay, and he watched dispassionately as she sobbed into her hands.

"Aye, I'll go into town. With any luck, I'll make it back today," Frederick said. He motioned for Slims to walk with him. Shorty walked beside them, but Dalton stood near Charlotte, waiting for her to calm enough so he could help her to her room in the bunkhouse.

Frederick paused halfway to the large house, his hands balled into his fists, his breath coming faster than usual, and his cheeks reddened. "I don't like this, Slims." He paused as he stared into his foreman's eyes. "Tell me the truth. Is anything she claims true?"

Slims shook his head. "She could be carryin' a babe, so that might be true. But it's not mine," he said emphatically. "I never touched her. There is no possible way that babe is mine." He looked at Shorty. "You know the hell I lived through out there."

Shorty nodded and let out a deep sigh. "I do. I feared, on the rare day I rode alone out on the range, that somethin' had happened."

Slims shook his head over and over again. "Never. I swear

on everything I hold holy." He paused and swallowed. "On my marriage to Davina, I never laid a hand on that woman. I wanted to throttle her numerous times for her insolence and her sass, but she's still breathin'."

Frederick sighed. "What a mess," he muttered. Casting an apologetic glance in Slims's direction, he muttered, "You know Sorcha will have informed Davina of Charlotte's arrival. And of her pronouncement."

"Dammit," Slims hissed. "All I wanted was a little time to settle in with my bride. To learn what that was like. Was that too much to ask?" He stormed off in the direction of the big house. After entering the house, he paused, taking a moment to calm his anger and to remind himself that none of this was Davina's fault. He needed to soothe her.

After poking his head into the kitchen and finding it empty, he walked down the hallway to Sorcha's sitting room. He paused, listening to Sorcha sing what sounded like a lament to him but which she would claim was a love song and then knocked. "Is Davina here?"

Sorcha continued to spin her wool, her gaze filled with concern as she beheld him. "Nae, she said she needed time to consider the news."

Slims saw the children asleep in the corner and kept his voice down, although he flushed with indignation. "You know as well as I do that that woman lies, Sorcha."

"Perhaps. But what I dinna understand is why she would claim such a thing when she had to ken we'd send for Helen?" She shook her head. "Thus I'm thinkin' part of her story must be true. She's with child, but not honest about who the father is, aye?"

Slims heaved out a breath. "You believe me? That I'm not the father?"

Sorcha flushed. "I canna lie, Slims. I had moments where I

doubted ye. An' where I felt disappointment in ye." She paused as she studied him, standing as though a supplicant in her bower. "But seein' ye standin' afore me miserable, an' knowin' how hard ye've avoided any an' all entanglements in the past, I dinna see ye takin' a wife when ye had so recently been involved with another woman. 'Tisn't like ye."

He suddenly found himself battling deep emotions at her expression of her faith in him. "Thank you, Miss Sorcha. Your belief in me is humbling."

"Ye're an honorable man, Slims. An' ye've earned my trust." She paused. "I fear my cousin's faith in ye is more fragile."

Slims swore under his breath and ran a hand through his hair. "I'll speak with her. And try to talk sense into her." He turned to leave, pausing to whisper, "If she only has faith after Helen proves my innocence, is that a trust worth valuing?" He slipped from the room before Sorcha could answer.

Rather than return to his cabin and confront Davina, he walked into the kitchen to pour himself a cup of coffee from the pot that was never allowed to be left empty. As he filled up his cup with the last of the coffee, he moved around the kitchen, making a fresh pot. Memories from the previous summer flitted through his mind. He remembered a persistent sensation of extreme aggravation and annoyance. The frustration that such a woman had been assigned to work the small homestead as the cook for him and Shorty. How many times had he grumbled to Shorty that they would have done better alone?

He sat with a *thud* as he thought through Charlotte's possible motives, and the only possible one was what he'd already accused her of. That she wanted him because he was a man of position on the ranch. For she'd never favored him when they were away from the big house.

Sighing, he took a sip of coffee and heard the sound of

bells as the sleigh left for town. Slims rose, glancing outside to see which horses Frederick had decided to use today and dropped his cup to the floor at the sight of Davina riding beside Frederick. Riding away from him.

D avina sat beside Frederick as the sleigh made its way to town. Although the day was brilliantly bright, and the mountains shone in the distance, she failed to see the day's beauty. Thankfully, Frederick seemed to understand her need for quiet, and the only sounds were that of the horses' hooves and the bells singing.

She clenched and unclenched her hands together in an attempt to dispel some of her tension, but it didn't work. Tugging the blanket tighter around her, she snuggled under its warmth, attempting to banish her memories of riding in the sleigh beside Slims. Of feeling cherished and safe. How could he have betrayed her like this? Now he would have a child with another woman, and that child would live. He would know what it would mean to be a father, and Davina would have no part in that experience.

Her breath caught as an overwhelming pain filled her. She had thought her first husband's disdain the worst torment she had to bear. How naive she was. This was a pain past bearing. To know her husband would have a child, and she never would ... She fought a sob as she attempted to push down her panic and despair.

She closed her eyes, reminding herself that they hadn't been married when the affair was purported to have occurred. He hadn't even known she, Davina, existed. However, her sense of betrayal did not abate. For he had never told her about Charlotte. Was that because Charlotte meant more than he wanted her to? Was he ashamed of his feelings for Charlotte? Davina shivered. Or was he ashamed of her?

Frederick made a sound in his throat, and she couldn't tell if he were making a noise for the horses or for her. He cast a quick glance in her direction. "You'll make yourself sick by imagining things. Only by speaking with Slims will you know the truth."

"How?" Davina gasped out. "How can I trust him?"

Frederick nodded, looking ahead to follow the road. "Aye, that's the crux of it. Trust." He paused. "Do you believe Sorcha and I have never hurt each other? We have," he said, regret lacing his voice. "And I've given thanks every day she trusts me not to ever hurt her intentionally again."

He paused for a few moments. "You want to know how to trust Slims? You do it by believing what you know to be true rather than by giving any credence to your fears." He pulled back on the reins so the horses slowed as they rounded a corner. "Fears only lead to heartache and disillusionment, Davina."

She shivered again, pulling the blanket tighter around her. However, the chill she felt was from deep within. "How do you get over feeling deceived?" she whispered.

"By not runnin' away from what scares you," he said with a wry smile. "Face Slims. Face Charlotte." He looked at her for a long moment. "Believe that you have the right to be happy, Davina. For, if you don't, you never will be."

Davina shuddered at his words, as though they were prophetic. For so long, she had thought she had little value. That her happiness was forfeited due to her inability to produce healthy babies who would survive more than a few months. Now she finally questioned those who would make her feel unworthy for all her sufferings. Why should she base her value off that alone?

"He doesn't want anything but you, Davina. The woman

who laughs and sings and fights with him. The real you, not the woman who attempts to know her place," Frederick murmured.

Davina nodded, lost in thought, already wishing she were riding back to the ranch, rather than away from it.

Slims walked to the barn with the milk cows, determined to find work to ease his tension now that Davina had left. He saw that most of the work had been completed, but he ensured none of the cows needed milking and fussed with spreading hay around. Tasks that didn't need to be completed but kept him busy.

Dalton joined him in the barn, and he leaned against a pole as he watched the big man work. "Why are you here, rather than talkin' to your wife?"

Slims slammed his pitchfork down and glared at his friend. "My wife hitched a ride into town with Fred. I don't know when she'll be back."

Dalton paled, and his eyes rounded at the news. "Slims," he said, as he shook his head, "what's goin' on?"

Pacing the small space between stalls, Slims shook his head. "Damned if I know. I thought that infernal woman was gone for good." He paused as he glared at Dalton, a man he'd known for years. "Tell me what you believe."

"After talkin' with you this morning, and seeing how Charlotte acted, I now realize I was a halfwit to believe her." His gaze held his unspoken apology. "That woman is desperate, and she's latched on to you in desperation," Dalton said with a shake of his head. "But I don't believe her claim. You're a man of honor, Slims. You'd never start up with your missus if you still had an attachment to Charlotte. And I know you." He paused. "If you had an attachment to Char-

143

lotte, you wouldn't have been so glad to see her go." He waved at Slims's pacing. "Look at how you're actin' because a woman you barely know has gone into town."

"Davina's special, Dalt," he whispered.

"Aye, which means Charlotte never was to you. And you wouldn't have entangled yourself with a woman who we all knew was an innocent. That's not who any of us are."

Slims let out a sigh of relief. "Then why were you so mad this mornin'?"

Dalton flushed. "She's a convincin' actress, and you weren't here. *She* was. I'm afraid it's easier to sow seeds of doubt than I thought it was." He shook his head again. "And then you returned, *married*." A smile formed, and he chuckled. "I never thought I'd see a person faint dead away, but she almost did last night." He frowned. "The problem is, she will most likely remain on the ranch until the thaw."

"Aye, an' Miss Sorcha has a big heart. She won't evict a heartless, homeless pregnant woman," Slims muttered. "No matter how much I'd like her to." He shared a rueful glance with Dalton.

"No you don't," Dalton said. "That's your anger talkin'. You would never want to harm a woman. That's not like you."

Slims nodded, but he feared Dalton was wrong. For he knew that, if Charlotte threatened his marriage, he could see harming her. He couldn't lose Davina. Not when he'd just found her.

~

News and Noteworthy

I magine my surprise, Dear Reader, to be subjected to a biased, ignorant, petulant tirade by a man who should have merited the town's respect. Instead Pastor Cruikshanks earned my pity and my fervent thanksgiving that such a man would no longer reside among us. For who among us should ever cast aspersions as Pastor Cruikshanks did last week? Who among us is without fault or sin?

I, for one, know I am grateful and delighted that such a fine woman as Davina MacQueen, now Mrs. Davina Slims, is a member of my family. She forsook her comfort, while also risking her life, to ensure a good man did not freeze to death in last week's horrible blizzard. To be so pilloried by a man of the cloth for an act of Christian charity is beyond comprehension.

My hope, Dear Reader, is twofold. First, that you are filled with a more charitable spirit than our recently departed pastor and are able, and eager, to welcome such a fine woman into our community. Second, I pray the new preacher is a more understanding and forgiving man. For I've come to realize we do not need more judgment raining down on us from the pulpit. We are in desperate need for more compassion.

∾

D avina wandered into the larger of the two mercantiles, the Merc, glancing at the fine cloths on display. She imagined buying a bolt of it and sewing new dresses for her and Sorcha, but she refrained from doing any more than lightly fingering the cloth. She reminded herself that, although such luxuries had been commonplace for her in her life in Scotland, they had never brought her lasting joy.

"Might I help you, Mrs. Slims?" Tobias Sutton asked.

She pivoted to face the proprietor, flushing at being caught ogling his fine merchandise. "Oh no," she breathed.

"I'm fine. Passin' time." She turned to leave, but Tobias gently gripped her arm.

"If you have time, missus, why don't you have a cup of tea with me? It seems to me you could use a place for quiet contemplation, away from family." He moved to the front of his store, flipped the sign to Closed, and motioned for her to follow him to the back room.

After she had settled on a chair, he made them a pot of tea and sat across from her at a table. "I dinna understand why ye are bein' kind to me," she protested.

Her words seemed to cause him to reflect a moment. "I knew a woman once, who looked and acted like you. Brave, but lost inside. She needed someone to listen and to give her wise advice. I fear she didn't find that."

"What happened to her?" Davina whispered.

"She betrayed all she loved and lost everything," Tobias murmured.

With quivering hands, Davina lifted her cup with both hands, as though knowing she'd dump the contents if she used just one hand. "I don't know what to do." She stared at him, her expression filled with desperation and terror. "I fear I've made the gravest of mistakes."

Tobias half smiled. "If you mean that you erred by marrying Slims, then rest assured that you haven't. He's one of the finest men I've ever met. Only finer are my nephews." He waited for her to say something more, and, when she remained quiet, he asked, "What would ever cause you to doubt?"

Her shoulders stooped, and she stared into the tea mug, as though too ashamed to meet his gaze. "A woman arrived at the ranch while we were in town. Makin' claims she's carryin' my husband's bairn." When he snorted his doubt, she glanced at him. "Why are ye certain she lies an' he doesna?"

Tobias crossed his arms over his chest, studying her. "It

146

doesn't matter what I say. What Frederick or Sorcha say. What my aunt and uncle say." He quieted for a moment. "What matters is what you know to be true, deep inside you. What does your heart tell you, Davina?"

She shook her head, tears coursing out. "I canna trust it."

"If there's one thing you can trust, it's that. For that is your truth, trying to speak to you." He gripped her hand. "What does it say?"

"That the woman is a liar. That she's tryin' to ruin my life, just as I have a chance at happiness again." She firmed her lips. "An' it makes me so angry!" By this time, she had set the mug down, and she swiped at her cheeks. "Because I'm lettin' her." Her voice held a sense of astonished understanding. "I'm lettin' her ruin what I have."

Tobias nodded. "You are." He slurped a sip of his tea. "I imagine Frederick is here to fetch Helen to prove the woman is a liar." He saw the truth in Davina's gaze. "Don't wait for Helen to confirm what you already know, Mrs. Slims. For, if you do, then Slims will always doubt your faith in him." He ducked his head, as though deep in thought, before murmuring, "Don't waste your second chance, Davina, for most of us aren't so fortunate as to ever be offered such a gift."

She paled at his words before nodding. "Aye. Thank ye, Mr. Sutton."

At a pounding on the back door, he rose. "Hello, Frederick," he said, as he stepped aside for Frederick to enter. "Davina and I were enjoying a cup of tea."

"You made her cry!" Frederick accused, glaring at Tobias. "Why must you always stir up trouble?"

"Frederick, nae," Davina murmured. "Mr. Sutton helped me confront my truth. He's a good man." She saw confusion and an aching regret in Frederick's gaze that she didn't understand. "Have ye found Helen?"

He nodded. "Yes, she and Warren will head out soon. If

we leave now, we have time to return tonight." He looked at Tobias. "Uncle," he said shortly, before marching out the back door.

"Uncle?" Davina breathed.

Tobias scratched at his head. "Yes. I'm his uncle. A man he still wishes he didn't have to claim as family."

Davina stood on her toes and kissed Tobias's cheek. "I thank ye for yer advice." She rushed past him to catch up to Frederick, leaving a dazed Tobias behind.

CHAPTER 8

Slims sat in his foreman's cabin, a home he'd only ever spent one night in, and waited for his wife to return. A place he'd only ever considered home since he had carried her over the threshold the day before. He closed his eyes as images of the previous night flashed through his mind. Of her lustrous hair, spread over the pillows, as she laughed up at him. At her flushed cheeks and the joy in her gaze. Of her curled beside him, sleeping peacefully in his arms. He rubbed at his chest, a deep ache settling within, at the thought she'd never look at him in the same way again.

He opened his eyes and stared at the stove and the crackling wood inside. He was intent on keeping it well fed so the cabin would be warm for her on her return. For he refused to believe she would not return to him. He did not know how he would survive if she didn't.

Clenching and unclenching his fists, he battled anger and a sense of impotence at not being able to allay her fears. Theirs was such a new relationship and her trust in him so fragile. He feared she would find it easier to believe the worst in him rather than having faith in him.

149

Leaning forward, he rested on his elbows, as he contemplated Frederick returning with Helen and Warren, for he knew Warren would insist on traveling with his wife. "What would that be like?" he murmured to himself. To have a relationship where the trust and the love ran so deep that there was no doubt. He had never thought to feel a soul-sickening envy, but he did. For he wanted that. And he feared he would never have the chance to earn it.

He forced himself to remain seated as the sound of sleighs arriving sounded in the yard. He knew Davina would go with Frederick and wait with Sorcha to hear what Helen said. Her trust in him would only be rebuilt with the proof of his innocence.

At the sound of the door scraping open, he sat tall and glared at whoever dared to enter his sanctuary. At the sight of his wife, he leaped to his feet, his hands clenching and unclenching again as he battled the urge to tug her into his arms. To run his hands over her and to ensure she was well. "Davina," he whispered. "I thought you'd go to the big house."

She shook her head, and he thought he discerned an embarrassed blush on her cheeks. "Nae," she said in so low a voice it was almost a whisper. "I wanted to see my husband." She bit her lip as she looked at him. "I needed to see him." She took a step toward him and then stood stock-still as he remained frozen in place. "Unless ye dinna want me here?"

He took the two steps separating them and pulled her into his arms. "Don't be foolish," he growled, as he held her close and lifted her off her feet a moment, earning a shriek. "God, I've missed you. And it's only been a few hours since I held you in my arms."

When he felt her freeze at his words, he settled her on the ground and released her. "Davina?"

She took a deep breath and stared deeply into his eyes. "I

have to ask ye, Simon. Is there any truth to what she said? To what she claims?"

He cupped her cheeks and shook his head. "No, Davina, no. I never touched her. I'll scream it to the moon and back, but I swear to you I didn't. I pro—"

She covered his mouth with her small hands and shook her head, a luminous smile bursting forth. "Nae, my Simon. Ye dinna have to protest and proclaim. If ye say ye were no' with her, I believe ye." She continued to look deeply into his eyes. "I trust ye."

He groaned and hauled her against his chest. "Oh, my darling, thank you," he rasped. He held her close for a few moments before whispering in her ear, "Why did you go to town?"

"I ... I was so afraid," she breathed. She bravely met his gaze when he eased her back so he could look deeply into her eyes. "I feared she would give ye what I never could."

Slims stared at her in stunned silence a moment. "A child?"

"Aye. An' I felt horribly inadequate." She shrugged and dropped her gaze to the floor.

"No, my darlin', no," Slims said in a passionate voice. He paused, waiting for her to meet his gaze again. "There is no one for me but you." He pulled her close again, his hands roving over her coat-covered body, and he growled with impatience to find her so covered in garments. He stilled his movements at the loud knocking on the door. "Yes?" he called out.

Shorty's voice said, "You're needed in the big house. You an' your missus."

Slims sighed, resting his forehead against hers. "I'm sorry, Dav. I wanted a little more time for the two of us. For me to show you that I mean what I say."

She smiled, standing on her tiptoes to give him a fleeting

kiss. "'Tis all right, Simon. I ken we'll have time tonight." Her flirtatious smile eased some of his worry, as he reached for his coat and hat, following her from the cabin to the main house.

~

Davina entered the big house, her hand in Slims's. Although she knew they still needed to discuss so much, a deep sense of peace pervaded her. She squeezed his hand as she saw an unknown woman sitting in a chair, alone and to one side of the two whispering groups gathered in the same room. She knew the woman had to be the mysterious Charlotte, who had made claims against her husband. Any sense of calm evaporated as a rage filled Davina at what this woman had attempted to do to her and Slims. At what she, Davina, had almost allowed Charlotte to do.

Taking a deep breath, she followed Slims to join Frederick and Sorcha, who each held one of the twins, while they talked quietly with Warren. "Helen?" Slims asked. The other small group consisted of Shorty, Dalton, and Dixon, and they kept a wide berth from Charlotte too.

"She's washing up, and then she will join us," Warren said. They stood near the doorway to Frederick's office and close to the crackling fire. Various lamps lit the room as night fell.

Davina watched as Slims glowered at the woman sitting in stunned silence across the room. Gripping his arm, she gave it a gentle tug to prevent him from storming over to her. "Nae, Slims," she murmured. "Now that I see her, somethin' more is goin' on. I dinna ken what, but she has the lost look of a woman near the verge of a collapse."

Slims paused and focused on her. "She's a hellion, Davina."

Frederick chuckled. "I used to think the same of Sorcha,"

152

he murmured, as he ran a hand down his wife's back. "I finally learned it was all just a shield to protect herself." He cast a glance across the room. "I wonder if Charlotte isn't like my wife."

Taking a deep breath, Slims shook his head. "No, she does not get to be exonerated for what she attempted to do. For the harm she tried to inflict on my marriage." He looked at his friends. "She does not deserve your understanding."

Sorcha gripped his arm, shaking her head, as she smiled softly at him. "Everyone deserves understandin', Slims. Although I fear there are times when our compassion is no' as great as it should be."

Davina rose on her toes and kissed his cheek. "Have faith, husband. I trust you. All will be well." She held his gaze, waiting until he nodded and relaxed under her unwavering stare and from her avowal. Her attention shifted to the woman who had just entered the room from the back hallway. "Helen."

Helen smiled to all of them, although her gaze was guarded. She glanced at Charlotte sitting in a near stupor and pursed her lips. "I know you have questions, but I'm uncertain I can answer them. I can't break the confidence of a patient." She met Slims's and Frederick's irate glowers. "I know you brought me here to answer questions, but she's my patient, not you."

Davina had stiffened at Helen's words. After a long moment, her grip on her husband's arm eased, and she smiled. "I admire ye, Helen. Ye are the definition of honorable. Few would have the temerity to stand up to a group of strangers, never mind their friends."

Helen shook her head. "No, they are my family. But I can't break my pledge."

With a nod, Davina focused on the woman sitting alone. After squeezing her husband's arm once more, she separated herself from their small group and approached the woman. "Ye're Charlotte, aye?" she asked, as she pulled a chair over to sit beside her. When the woman raised terror-filled eyes, Davina sucked in her breath. "Who hurt ye, lass?"

Charlotte shook her head, her gaze returning to study the floorboards.

"Why would ye make such a claim against my husband?" she whispered.

"I didn't know he was married," she whispered. "And then I heard it was a marriage of necessity. I thought he could annul it and marry me."

Davina sent a quick glance in her husband's direction, filled with heat, admiration, and desire. "Aye, 'twas of necessity, but we would have eventually married." She paused, waiting to see if Charlotte would say anything more. "May Helen speak with us?"

Charlotte shrugged. "It doesn't matter. The truth will come out eventually." Tears leaked out, and she sat with stooped shoulders.

Looking at Helen, Davina saw that Helen had heard Charlotte's quiet words. Rather than join her husband, family, and friends, Davina remained seated by Charlotte. Slims moved to stand beside her, his large palm resting on her shoulder, while Warren and Helen sat on one settee and Frederick and Sorcha the other. Dalton, Shorty, and Dixon remained standing.

Helen took a deep breath. "I believe I was called to the ranch to determine if Charlotte was expecting a child and, if possible, to discern how soon she was to have this child." She cleared her throat. "I'm afraid I can't answer that question."

At the huff of incredulity from Frederick and the swears from the ranch hands, Warren rose from his seat and glared them into silence. Helen flushed and gripped her husband's hand. "Charlotte was expecting a child, but she no longer is."

Her blush intensified as she studied the pattern of her checkered wool skirt. "Forgive me. I'm not used to discussing such matters with men."

Frederick waved away her concern. "Are you telling me that Charlotte was pregnant but lost the child, and was still trying to convince Slims it was his and that he had to marry her to prevent scandal?"

Helen paused as she thought through what he said. "I can't answer to motive. All I can say is that she was expecting and no longer is. I can't answer to how far along she was before she lost the baby. I have very little to offer."

Slims cleared his throat before the cacophony of complaints could restart. "I disagree," he said in his low, commanding voice. "You have given us—me—quite a lot. Your word is never to be discredited, as you are honorable. Thus, we know this woman is not pregnant. There is no urgency for her to wed." He paused. "I swear on all I hold most precious in my life, my wife and the memory of my family, that I never touched Charlotte." Davina's sharp inhalation brought a rueful smile to his lips. "You all must decide if you believe a woman who has shown herself to be a liar or if you believe me."

Frederick nodded. "You, of course, Slims." His gaze flitted to Charlotte, who swayed ever-so-slightly from side to side and seemed unaware of what was occurring around her. "However, something happened, and we need to discover what did."

The ranch hands nodded. "Boss is right. Someone harmed her, and it ain't right. Miss Charlotte was always full of piss and vinegar, and now she's as meek as Sunset," Dixon said, referring to the docile milk cow. He scratched at his head as he stared at her.

Dalton studied her and shook his head. "Ain't right."

Helen spoke up. "I fear she has lost a fair amount of

blood. I know she has done harm with her claims, but she would benefit from remaining here on the ranch for a few more days, as she recovers. If it is acceptable, Warren and I will remain to ensure she recovers as well as possible."

Frederick smiled wryly. "If you want a vacation each winter on the ranch around the time of your anniversary, you only have to ask. The caretaker's cottage is still free."

Warren chuckled and nodded. "Thanks, Fred."

Helen rose to approach Charlotte and, with Davina's help, eased her patient to her feet. "Come, Charlotte. You must rest."

"Use the room on the first floor. A bed is still in there, and the bairns dinna need every room in the house," Sorcha said with a soft kiss and caress to Mairi's head.

Davina walked beside Charlotte, her shoulder under the dazed woman's arm. With each step, it seemed Davina carried more of the other woman's weight. "Is she verra ill?" Davina whispered.

Helen gave a jerk of her head, settling Charlotte into the bed. After checking for fever, she sat beside her. Davina pulled out another chair to join the healer. "She's ailing," Helen whispered. "I can't determine if it is due to blood loss or spiritual malaise."

Davina let out a stuttering breath. "The loss of a child injures ye in ways ye canna imagine."

Helen stared at her with curiosity, although she didn't ask any questions. "I have seen that, too many times to count."

Davina sat beside Charlotte on the bed, holding her hand. "Ye are safe here, Charlotte," she whispered. "Whatever ye are runnin' from, the men here are good an' honorable, an' they willna allow ye to come to harm."

Charlotte focused on her, her sherry-colored eyes dulled with disillusionment. "No one is strong enough to save me. I was a fool to return here." She curled in on herself, a hand low over her belly, as she closed her eyes, as though shutting out everyone and everything she could not see.

"Charlotte," Davina murmured, running a soothing hand down her back. When the woman did not respond, Davina sighed and shared a look with Helen.

Helen shrugged and motioned for Davina to follow her from the room. "Don't worry. I'll be here a few days. If she has a physical illness, I'll work to ensure she does not worsen. If her spirit is broken, I'm afraid there is little I can do to mend it. She'll have to find the inner strength to overcome what torments her."

Slims approached Warren and Frederick, who motioned them to follow him into his office. After closing the door behind him, Frederick sat in the chair behind his desk; Warren settled into the chair in front of it, and Slims stood to the side, his arms crossed over his strong chest. Slims's brows furrowed as he studied the two men who he thought were good friends and noted the sudden tension in the room.

"What's the matter, Warren?" Frederick asked with a sigh. He had circles under his eyes from sleepless nights with the twins, although he did not have to worry about the success of the ranch this year. It had been a mild winter.

"How long will you allow Charlotte to remain on the ranch?" Warren asked.

With a shrug, Frederick yawned and sat back in his chair. "As long as she needs to. She's harmless, and I believe Davina feels the same." His gaze flickered to Slims, who remained stone-faced.

"Slims?" Warren asked. "Is that how Davina feels?"

"I don't know. She doesn't like the woman, or she didn't before we entered the big house tonight. But Dav's compassionate, and she'll have sympathy for her, even if Charlotte doesn't deserve it."

Warren stared at Frederick with a warning look in his eyes. "If Charlotte is to stay here, you must consider that one of your men will become entangled with her." He paused as though searching for words, an uncommon occurrence for the lawyer.

Frederick froze at Warren's warning and then sat forward in his chair. Tilting his head to one side, Frederick stared at Warren, as though he were a stranger. "You know my men are honorable," he said in a low voice, all the more potent because of its deep timbre and volume. "Over and over, they have shown their respect to every woman who has arrived at this ranch, seeking refuge. How dare you imply they will treat Charlotte any differently?" He slammed his hand onto his desk, leaning forward, his blue eyes blazing as he challenged the lawyer.

Smiling, Warren let out a huff of air. "Your men want wives. And they aren't afraid of trying to sweet-talk every woman who comes here into being their bride. If I'm not correct, one of your men even tried to court Sorcha away from you." He looked at Slims, who grunted in agreement. "And I would bet another attempted to ingratiate himself into Davina's good graces and away from Slims." He nodded as he saw the truth in each man's eyes. "I would never doubt the honor of your men. Nor would I believe they'd get a woman with child and abandon her. Hell, they'd be too excited to have a woman to ever let her go."

"We're not mindless beasts," Slims snapped, standing tall, his arms now tightly crossed over his chest.

"Of course not. But you're men who've spent enough time alone without a woman's gentle presence. You're smart enough to hold on to a good woman when you find her. And wise enough to know a good woman doesn't enter your life very often."

"Charlotte's proven she's not a good woman," Slims said.

Shaking his head, Warren sighed. "No, she hasn't. She's proven she's human. And vulnerable. Did my wife prove herself unworthy by going to the Boudoir? Did Sorcha prove unlovable because she raced from the livery and broke her leg? Is Davina less worthy because she fled Scotland, defying her family's wishes and imposing on you?"

Warren looked at the men, seeing their instant denials to his questions. He pointed to the living room and, by extension, the room where Charlotte was settling in with his wife and Davina. "That woman—no matter what you feel about her right now—has the ability to provoke discord."

"I've never denied refuge from someone who needs it," Frederick said. "And I won't start now."

"The men know better than to take advantage of a defenseless woman," Slims said in a soft voice. "And every man in that room tonight saw a vulnerable woman on the verge of collapse."

Warren rubbed at his head. "Stop being obtuse! In a month, maybe six weeks, the thaw will start, and drifters will return. Not all of them will be good men. Not all of them will be men you know well and can trust, as you can trust Shorty, Dalton, and Dixon."

Slims rocked back on his heels, a look of deep comprehension in his gaze. "Ah, I understand," he whispered. "You're tryin' to get us to ensure she's taken before the drifters return," Slims said. "In a very roundabout lawyerly way."

Frederick groaned and flopped back in his chair. "I'm too tired for this," he muttered, rubbing at his eyes. "Speak plainly, Warren."

Warren bit his lip and shook his head. "Because I'm a

lawyer, I can't." He looked into Frederick's eyes. "Because I'm *her* lawyer, I can't." He closed his eyes. "Save her, Fred. Find one of the men you trust to save her. Before it's too late. Before …" He broke off and sighed, tugging at his hair in frustration.

Slims stiffened. "That's why you weren't elated I was marryin' Davina," he breathed. "Because you'd already sent Charlotte out here, expectin' I'd be here to wed her." Slims took a menacing step in Warren's direction, only stilling at Frederick's warning.

"Slims." Fred shook his head. After a moment, he focused on Warren. "Why not just tell me that she's in trouble and that one of my men must marry her?" Frederick asked again, suddenly wide awake and any fatigue a distant memory.

Warren closed his eyes and, for the first time that either Slims or Frederick had ever seen him, appeared defeated. "I can't. I shouldn't have said what I said tonight." He stared at them with unfettered rage mixed with an irrepressible despair. Whispering, he said, "I hoped you'd come to the decision that she must be protected on your own. And that my advice would never be a part of that decision. For it can't be."

Frederick tapped his index finger on his desk as he studied Warren, while Slims watched him as though meeting him for the first time. "I'll speak with the men. And I'll speak with Charlotte. No matter what you recommend, Warren, I'll never force a woman to marry against her will."

Slims grunted his agreement.

"Convince her," Warren said in a tone that brooked no argument. "Or you'll be planning a funeral, rather than a wedding."

❧

160

S lims opened the door to the small cabin, his pent-up breath easing at the sight of Davina rocking in the chair in front of the fire, softly singing to herself. The tension seeped away as her lilting voice crooning in her native Gaelic washed over him, freeing him of his worries and filling him with unfettered joy. "Forgive me for not being here to build up the fire." His breath caught as she looked over her shoulder at him, her song breaking off at his quiet interruption.

"I ken ye have work to do, Simon. An' today has no' been a normal day." She stared at him for such a long time, he shifted from foot to foot. "You'll join me, aye?"

He smiled. "Aye." After shutting and latching the door, he settled in his comfortable chair, absently holding out his hand to hold hers. He almost grabbed it back but made himself keep it extended to see what she would do. He heard her huff of surprise when she noted it and then the softness of her palm as her hand clasped his. Another ache in his soul eased at her quiet acceptance of his affection. "Thank you."

He squeezed her hand, hoping to impart comfort and reassurance, as he sat in his gentleman's chair. However, when he heard her sniffle, he looked at her with concern. "Davina? What's the matter?"

"How can ye bear the sight of me?" she whispered. "I doubted ye." She sat with lowered head, as though she had much to repent.

Slipping from his chair, he knelt in front of her, his large hands clasping her knees. "No ..." He sighed and broke off his protestations. "Yes, you did." He met her tormented gaze. "And I won't lie. It hurt, Dav. Almost as bad as anything I've ever felt in my life. I'd hoped we were building something good and strong between us."

Her eyes shimmered with unshed tears. "We are, Simon.

Please," she breathed, her hand shaking as she caressed his cheek.

Smiling, he turned his head into her soft touch. "God, that feels like heaven," he whispered. "I feared you'd never touch me again, at least not willingly." He met her stricken gaze. "What is it?"

"I ken I told ye that I trust ye, an' I do," she said, as she took a deep breath. "But do ye trust me?"

"What?" he asked, his hold on her knees tightening. "What on earth do you mean, woman?"

A tear trickled down her cheek as she brushed at his eyebrow. "I left ye today, rather than talk with ye. I ran." Her voice lowered to a barely audible pitch, filled with her remorse and her agony. "I'm so sorry."

"Watchin' you leave about gutted me today." He swiped at her cheeks. "I worked like a madman, and I prayed you'd return to me." He fidgeted with a piece of her unbound hair. "Where did you go? What did you do in town?"

She shrugged. "Frederick left to find Helen, an' I realized I didna have any desire to see my family an' explain I'd been a fool." She flushed. "I ken they'd understand I have a temper, as I've been told they have it too, but I didna need to show them so soon after meetin' me what a simpleton I was." She flinched when she saw the ire in his gaze.

"Don't, Dav," he said in a low, warning-filled voice. "Don't talk about yourself like that. You aren't a simpleton, and you aren't a fool. You felt betrayed." His voice was filled with remorse. "I'm sorry."

"But ye didna betray me, husband," she said, her eyes lit with an impassioned fervor. "Charlotte did."

"Yes," he said with a sigh. "For whatever reason, she did." He paused a moment. "What did you do in town?"

"I spoke with Mr. Sutton. Did ye ken he's Frederick's uncle?"

Slims sat back on his heels, stunned and struck dumb for a moment.

Davina watched her husband's reaction, whispering, "Was it wrong to speak with him? To have tea with the man?"

"You had tea with him?" he asked. He pushed away and rose, pacing a few steps before sitting in his chair beside her again.

Davina turned her rocking chair to the side, so she partially faced her husband. "I dinna understand, Simon. Why are ye so upset?"

"How did Frederick react when he found you there?" Slims asked.

Her brows furrowed, and she deflated a little. "Upset and worried that Mr. Sutton had made me cry." She rested her arm on Slims's hand as he tensed. "He didna! I promise. He helped me see the truth of the situation."

Shaking his head, Slims let out a deep breath. "To think Tobias has learned from his mistakes," he muttered.

"What do ye mean, Simon?" she whispered. "Why was Frederick so angry at his uncle? An' why did I no' ken he was Frederick's uncle?" She rubbed at her temple.

"Many years ago, Tobias ran away with Fred's mother, his cousin's wife, shattering Fred's family." Slims closed his eyes. "Everyone was miserable, but the misery didn't end with her departure." He met Davina's shocked gaze. "It took a long time for Frederick to learn to trust again. It took Miss Sorcha." He stared into her stunned gaze for a long moment. "What did Tobias say, Davina?"

She reached forward and clasped his hand. "He told me to trust my heart," she whispered, looking down. "An' I realized I was angry. Angry that I was allowin' this woman I didna ken to steal my happiness without a fight. For ye are very much worth fightin' for." She flushed when she saw the deep emotions in his gaze. "An', just before Frederick

163

arrived, Mr. Sutton advised me no' to squander my second chance."

Slims smiled. "I hope you take his advice," he murmured. "And listen to your heart."

"I'm here, aye?" she asked with hope in her gaze.

He groaned, his large hands reaching out to grip her arms. "Come here, love. Let me hold you." He sighed with relief when she moved with eagerness to climb onto his lap. When he had settled her and had wrapped his arms around her, he sighed with pleasure. "I never want you far from me."

She nestled her head under his chin. "I agree." She played with a button on his shirt before whispering, "I have to ask ye a question." At his mumble to ask whatever she wanted, she eased back to look into his eyes before blurting out, "Who was the woman ye wanted, but she had eyes for someone else?" She flushed with mortification. "When I heard about Charlotte, all I could think was she was the woman, an' she'd come back for ye."

Slims groaned and rested his head against the back of his chair. "No, never her. You can ask Dalton about this conversation. He'll vouch for me."

"No, I'm askin' my husband. Tell me." She clasped his face between her palms.

"I was referrin' to Miss Sorcha. She had a fire an' a sweetness about her, but it was obvious from almost the moment she came to the ranch that she was destined to marry Fred. Dalton joked with me one day about marryin', and I told him that I would only consider it if Miss Sorcha had a cousin. I never expected you to arrive."

She gaped at him as a tear coursed down her cheek.

"But that was a few years ago," she whispered.

"Aye, an' nothin' happened between the two of us. Nothin' except friendship. Your cousin is a remarkable woman and is to be admired. She only has eyes for Frederick." He paused. "I had hoped, if a relative of hers were to arrive, that she'd be like Sorcha. Loyal. Kind. Fiery. Lovely." He smiled. "And she is."

"Simon," she whispered through a tear-thickened throat. "I dinna deserve such praise."

"You do, darlin'. Oh, you do." He pulled her close, his hands stroking her back. "Do you know the pride I felt when you burst into the cabin today, intent on seeing me? When you proclaimed you didn't need Helen's proof?" He shuddered. "I thought I'd burst with joy."

"I ... I care for ye," she whispered. "More than I thought possible."

He chuckled. "Good. Because I ... I care for you too," he murmured, as he kissed her softly. "I have since we began our cooking lessons together. All I wanted was to hear you speak or sing or spend another second in your presence. Even though it was torture too."

"Oh, Simon," she whispered. "I never kent. I thought ye were annoyed with me."

He chuckled. "Annoyed with how much I wanted you. Annoyed with the belief I was to again be denied a woman who I could adore." He kissed her head. "I tried to stay away as much as possible, but, once you were cooking meals without my help, I counted down each minute until it was time for supper so I could see you again."

"Oh, Simon," she breathed, her eyes luminous as she gazed at him reverently.

"I dreaded the thaw," he said, as he kissed his way down her neck, smiling as she arched into his touch.

"Why?" she gasped.

"Because I knew we'd get a new cook, and I'd be in the bunkhouse with the men. I'd only see you in passing. And the thought of not having time with you every day ..." He shook his head and then turned his cheek into her palm. "Will you come to bed, darlin'? Let me show you all the ways I missed you?"

An incandescent smile burst forth, and she nodded, squealing with delight when he rose, carrying her in his strong arms to their bed and the pleasure to be found within.

CHAPTER 9

"Oh, Davina," Sorcha said, as she sat beside her cousin in Sorcha's rear sitting and work room the following afternoon. The twins played in the large crib in the corner, entertaining each other as Sorcha worked. "I was so worried when you left with Frederick. An' I kent Slims was too." She gripped Davina's hand. "Last night it seemed like you reconciled. Ye seemed at peace when ye stood beside him an' that ye are no' mad at him anymore. For ye did no' come to the big house, seeking refuge." Sorcha's eyes glowed with concern and hope.

Davina smiled and leaned forward into Sorcha's ready embrace. "'Tis wondrous, Sorcha. He was waitin' for me, an' I asked him to forgive me. I was a fool, an' I didna ken what to do with my powerful fear of him lovin' another woman."

Sorcha bit her lip. "He's had a past, aye?"

"Aye," Davina said with a laugh, "but 'tisn't one includin' Charlotte. An' I ken now, if I want to have a good relationship with my husband, I must no' be meek an' passive. I must show how much I care for him."

Sorcha crinkled up her nose, her hands fisting in a

mound of soft, rough wool. "*Care* for him? Nae, ye *care* about gettin' a good sleep each night. Ye *care* for those ye dinna ken well." She leaned forward, her gaze filled with a heartfelt fervency. "Ye love, Davina. Love yer husband an' yer family."

Flushing and then paling, Davina sat back in her chair, as a subtle trembling worked through her. "I ... I'm afraid I'm no' good at that kind of emotion. Carin's about the limit of what I can offer."

Sorcha made a deep sound of disgust. "Does Slims ken ye'll never love him? That ye'll only care for him?" she challenged, her gaze aflame with passionate outrage. "Ye canna go through life hidin' from what ye want an' what ye feel, Davina." She paused as she saw anguish in her cousin's gaze, her anger seeping out of her as fast as it had come. "I understand fear. But I also learned, if I did not show my husband, an' tell him, of my love, that I would hurt him in ways I couldna imagine." She let out a deep breath. "In ways I couldna bear to hurt him."

Davina sighed, her gaze desolate. "Love's always betrayed me," she whispered, flushing with embarrassment. "I dinna remember a time I was loved for me." She shook her head, closing her eyes, as she envisioned a long ago time. She murmured, "That isna true. Aunt Mairi loved me as I was. No' as she wished I'd be. An' 'twas was such a gift." She sniffled, meeting Sorcha's gaze, and whispered, "My da told me, when she died, I couldna mourn such a woman, an' that love was a wasted emotion. An' that her love had been wasted on me."

"Oh, Davina," Sorcha whispered, as tears trickled down her cheek. "That was his twisted truth. No' yers. Ye ken?"

"It became mine." Davina swiped at her cheeks. "For no one loved me in my da's house." She closed her eyes. "Or in my first husband's house."

Sorcha squeezed her hand and smiled reassuringly at her.

"I ken ye're wrong. Frederick came home with a pile of mail for us, an' mixed in the post was a letter for ye. From Scotland. I ken no one would have written ye if they did no' care." Her triumphant smile burst forth as she pulled out a letter from her pocket.

Davina's hand shook as she traced her da's handwriting. "My da," she breathed. "I wonder how he kent where to find me?" she whispered. After taking two deep breaths, she slit open the envelope and extracted the paper inside, her expression one of hope and yearning. Within a few moments, the hope had been vanquished, and she gasped for breath and paled as the paper shook in her hands. She stuffed the letter back into the envelope, wrinkling it and nearly ripping the envelope.

"Davina?" Sorcha asked. "Is all well?"

"Merely a letter from my da," Davina croaked out. "Informin' me that he's a wee bit displeased by my actions." She stood up so abruptly she knocked over her chair. "If ye'll excuse me?" She raced away, tripping from the room in her haste.

D avina stumbled onto the front porch of Sorcha's home. Rather than the impressive mountains in the distance, her gaze saw the tidy row of homes abutting the peaceful harbor of her hometown, Portree, Scotland. She recalled neighbors calling out to her, people who had always seemed friendly. Did they pity her as her da did? Had they secretly thought Davina unlovable too?

Swiping at her cheeks, Davina walked with faltering steps to her cabin, *my home*, she whispered to herself, and curled into her rocking chair. After stoking the fire, she opened the envelope again with a shaking finger, hoping she had missed another missive from her mother. Some soft words of caring from the woman who had raised her. Swearing under her breath when it cut into her soft skin, Davina sucked on her bleeding finger, her fingers searching and turning the envelope over until it was empty, but only her da's missive filled the envelope. Against her will, her gaze unerringly roved over the letter from Scotland, as she read it again and then again.

A pervasive dread and disillusionment settled into her soul as her da's words settled deep inside. Words he had implied in the past but now so clearly expressed. "Oh, how foolish of me," she whispered. "I should have kent I'd never receive their support." She brushed at her cheeks, but the tears continued to fall in a steady stream.

Dropping the letter to the floor, she curled into the rocking chair, her arms wrapped tightly around her middle. Why would the people here act like they cared for her? How could they be so cruel as to give her false hope? Her mind turned to her husband, Slims. How was she to face him? If her own parents couldn't love her, how could anyone else?

Slims entered his cabin, a sigh of relief and pleasure escaping him at the sight of Davina. He still had trouble believing she was here. That she wouldn't disappear like a dream. "How was your day, darlin'?" he asked, as he hung up his hat and coat and approached her to stroke a hand down her arm.

Rather than the warm teasing smile he had expected, she sat, staring dully into the fire, barely noticing his appearance. "Why do ye lie?" she asked in a low confrontational voice.

"Lie?" Slims asked, rocking back onto his heels. "I don't understand what you mean."

She glared up at him. "Why do ye lie by calling me words like *love* an' *darlin'*?" She looked at him scornfully. "I ken ye have no real regard for me."

Slims froze under her verbal barrage, slowly lowering to his haunches, so he was near eye level with her. "Dav, what happened today? When I left this morning, everythin' was perfect between us."

"Aye, because I was willin' to believe a lie," she snapped. "A lie that ye could ever be content with me."

He rose, his face flushing and his hands fisting as he glared at her. No longer filled with tenderness, his confused, angry gaze clashed with hers. "I was content. And I thought you were content with me."

"*Content*," she whispered, her voice choked with tears. "'Tis a worse word than *care*." She sniffled. "But then I should have kent better than to expect anythin' different from a man who spends his days with animals."

Slims stiffened. "You knew who I was and what I do before you married me. It didn't seem to bother you then."

"Desperation breeds its own form of madness, aye?" she asked.

Breathing heavily, his hands clenching and unclenching at his sides, Slims demanded, "Are you saying you aren't satisfied? That you're upset you married me?"

She stared at him, shaking her head over and over, as an air of desolation swirled around them.

"Answer me!" he roared.

She turned away, curling into the rocking chair, her arms wrapped around her legs, quietly sobbing.

Swearing, Slims spun away, yanking on his hat and coat before marching outside and slamming the door. Deep breaths didn't calm the roiling emotions inside, and he trudged the short distance to the big house. When he entered, he heard the cacophony of delighted voices in the kitchen, wincing at the thought of having to join them. Instead he approached Frederick's office.

He entered, sitting in a chair in front of Frederick's desk, his gaze unfocused, as the argument played over and over in his mind. He couldn't figure out what went wrong or how he should have acted differently. He jerked when a hand clasped him on his shoulder.

"Slims," Frederick murmured, "it's not like you to sit in the dark and to ignore time with the men."

"I've never been married before," he muttered.

Frederick lit a lamp and sat beside Slims, rather than behind his desk. "What happened?"

With a dazed voice, Slims murmured, "I honestly don't know. I thought we were happy." He swallowed. "I was happy this mornin' when I left. How could she not have been? What did I miss? What did I do?" he asked, his hand clenching his thighs as he shook his head in despair.

With a sigh, Frederick gripped Slims around the nape. "Davina has fears. We all know that. I suspect you know more about them than anyone." When Slims remained quiet, Frederick murmured, "Sorcha gave her a letter today from Scotland. It was from her father. And from what Sorcha told me about Davina's reaction, he wasn't kind in what he wrote."

"A letter?" Slims asked. "How could a letter have ruined what we were startin' to have?"

Frederick let out a small laugh. "You'd be surprised what can disrupt your peace. I never know what will disturb Sorcha. But she trusts me enough now to tell me, rather than act out." He met Slims's devastated gaze. "I fear Davina hasn't had the time to learn to fully trust you yet, Slims."

Slims nodded, before whispering, "And that hurts almost as much as anythin' she said." He took a deep breath and rose. "Thanks, Fred."

~

After hours in the barn, where he spent the time sitting on a pile of hay and reliving all his encounters with Davina, he rose. He was chilled to his marrow, but he knew it had more to do with the loss of Davina's esteem than the cold temperature inside the barn.

After easing open the cabin door, he entered on soundless feet. With a quick glance, he saw his wife asleep on their bed, a pillow hugged to her chest, as though she missed having him beside her. His jaw clenched in anger and a deep remorse. After tugging off his boots, he approached her in stocking feet, pausing when he heard a small scraping sound on the floor as his feet rubbed against something. Bending over, he discovered a piece of paper.

With a glance at a sleeping Davina, he moved to the stove and lit a lamp. Sitting in his chair, he rapidly read the missive, his jaw tightening the more he read.

D *avina,*

I shall not call you darling daughter *ever again. For how could I proclaim you thus after you have betrayed everyone and everything that has sheltered and encouraged you? But you, you selfish, greedy, pathetic excuse for a daughter, never thought of anyone but yourself. I should have known I was cursed when your mother gave me a daughter. I should have known I was cursed when you mourned your worthless aunt Mairi with such fervency. I should have known I was cursed when you couldn't even keep a single bairn alive, thus endangering our alliance with the MacDonalds.*

Instead I continued to hope you would keep your part of the bargain. A well-respected husband, generous support for your family, and a comfortable home for you. Why should you believe

173

you deserve more? Why should you have the temerity to turn your back on everything this family has worked so hard for?

Did you believe Mairi's bastard child would take you in? Would love you? That you would find a better life than the life I worked to ensure you had with your second MacDonald husband? You are a fool to believe anyone would ever love you. Your curse is to never realize just how unlovable you are and always will be.

You are a disgrace and a discredit to the family MacQueen. When I am asked, I reply I have no daughter. She is dead. For you are. Never return, for no one misses you, and no one ever wants to see you again. And be under no illusion. No one is coming after you for that would infer you are precious or valued, and you are neither.

Baldwin MacQueen

"**B**astard," Slims breathed, reading it over once more, before his gaze landed on his wife. With the lamp lit, he could discern dried tear tracks down her cheeks, and his gut clenched at the thought of the pain she had suffered upon reading her father's disparaging words. Slims's anger flared again that she had lashed out at him, rather than seeking solace from him.

After stoking the fire, he picked up his chair and moved it to the side of the bed, where he sat to watch over his wife. He knew it would be a sleepless night for him, as too many emotions had been roiled and too much remained unanswered.

Her words, *desperation breeds its own form of madness,* continued to play, over and over, in his mind. Was that all she had felt when she had married him? Desperation? He rested his head against the back of his chair, closing his eyes as he remembered their recent wedding. The feeling of an abiding joy filled him as he recalled her walking toward him with a shy smile. Had he mistaken pleasure and hope in her gaze for desperation and a resignation with her fate? Shaking his head, he refused to believe he had been so wrong. Like him, Davina had not sought marriage, but she had appeared eager to create a life with him.

Uncertainties continued to plague him. And, beneath it all, a deep, resounding resentment toward her took root. He tried to fight it. However, as he stared at her, a bitterness filled him that she had believed one word of her father's vile letter rather than trusting in what they were building. Rather than seeking comfort from Slims, she had attempted to prove her father's words true. He sat, through the darkest hours of the night, watching her sleep, wondering if he could possibly overcome her lack of faith in him.

S lims groaned, arching his back as he woke. He stretched his arms overhead and groaned again as his muscles protested the night he'd spent in the chair. His movements froze when he saw Davina watching him. "How long have you been awake?" he rasped, clearing his voice of its rustiness.

"No' long," she whispered. "Why did ye no' join me in bed?" she asked in an abashed voice.

Leaning forward, he rested his elbows on his knees. "Why would I, Dav?" he asked. "You made it plain last night that you have little regard for me or our marriage."

"Nae," she whispered. "That is nae true." She waved her hand around, as though that explained what happened.

He waited, but she remained quiet. He rose, ignoring her protests at him moving away from her, and snatched the letter from the small table. Waving it at her, he said, "I read this last night. I found it illuminatin.'"

She paled as she sat up and reached forward to snatch it from him. He pulled it away from her, keeping it out of her hands.

"I was shocked and saddened by what I read," he said in a low, emotion-laden voice. "But I was more upset that you wouldn't tell me the truth."

Davina shrugged. "That is my truth."

He flushed and shook the sheet of paper from side to side. "There is precious little truth in this letter, Davina. I don't recall one thing he wrote that wasn't a lie."

She gaped at him, tears streaming down her cheeks.

"Never use my feelings against me again, Davina. That's cruel and unfeeling and unjust. It's something the man who fathered you would do. Not you. Never you." He stormed from the cabin, ignoring the tears cascading down her cheeks. He paused on the stoop of the small cabin, taking deep breaths, as he allowed the rage to seep from him. In its wake, all he felt was a searing agony and sadness. For himself and for his wife. He thought about his family, his loving father. He couldn't imagine receiving such a letter from his pa. How would he bear it?

With another deep breath, he turned on his heel and reentered the cabin, rushing to her side, as he saw her sobbing on their bed with such intensity that she nearly hyperventilated. "Breathe, love," he coaxed, as he eased her into his arms and settled with his back against the wall and her on his lap, easing her head onto his shoulder. Soon the cloth of his shirt was soaked by her tears, but he ignored everything except her misery. He hated that he had added to it by his own outburst. Although he had thought it a righteous outburst, he realized nothing was worth causing her one moment's worth of pain. "*Shh*, love," he murmured, "all will be well."

"How?" she stuttered out. "I … hurt ye. An' ye'll never forgive me."

He held her even closer and kissed the top of her head. "Aye, you did, and I will," he whispered. "I imagine you'll hurt me many more times in the next forty years." He said a silent prayer that he would be gifted with so much time with her. "I'll hurt you too. Like I just did by leaving you in anger, when you needed me to soothe you."

"You *caaaan*no' excuse what I said to ye last night, Simon," she choked out. "I said unforgiveable things."

He closed his eyes, as he thought through her words, his arms tightening around her. "Almost unforgiveable," he murmured, kissing her head again. "If you meant what you said, then I agree." His body tensed, as he waited for her to speak. However, she remained quiet. "Dav?"

"I'm sorry, Simon," she whispered, pushing up to meet his shuttered gaze. "Nae," she stammered, as her hands rose to clasp his hard jaw, abrading the day's worth of stubble. "Nae." She pushed him down, when he would have sat up, a smile bursting forth at the evidence of his care of her as he would not thrust her aside. He would not do anything that would lead to her harm. "Nae," she said one last time.

"I don't understand," he said in a soft voice, his emotionless gaze replaced by one of desperation and sadness. "Dav?"

"I did no' mean what I said. I lost myself to my da's words. Words I'd heard most of my life. Words I came to believe as true as any gospel." She choked on a sob, as she rested in his arms. "An' I believed his truths again. No' my own."

Slims was quiet, as he contemplated a lifetime of such abuse. Any resentment he had clung to evaporated as he realized the depths of despair she must have felt at receiving such a letter. He palmed her cheek, letting out a stuttering sigh of relief when she turned her cheek into his palm. "And not mine."

A tear trickled down her cheek. "What is yer truth?"

He smiled with a desperate tenderness, his fingers playing in her silky golden hair. "You are precious. A treasure I never thought to find. A gift I fear I am unworthy of." He kissed her cheek. "But I'm too selfish to ever give you up." Some of the tension in his shoulders eased at the wonder in her eyes. "And I give thanks every day for you, Dav. Don't let anyone sully what we have. Please."

"I'll try, Simon," she whispered as she fell forward into his strong arms. "I promise."

He wrapped his arms around her, rocking her side to side, wishing for an instant he could meet her father and insist he apologize to Davina. That Slims could show the man just how loveable his daughter was. And, just as quickly, Slims dismissed the idea, for he'd have to implore Bears to hide the body deep in the woods. There was no possible way Slims could meet the man who had caused his wife so much pain and not do him bodily harm. After a long moment, he breathed, "That's all I ask, my love."

~

For the next month, an uneasy truce existed between them. Davina continued to cook for all of them and to spend time with Sorcha in Sorcha's private room. Charlotte rarely ventured out of her room, although her only illness now was a deep emotional malaise. While Davina suspected Charlotte needed to be urged to leave her room and to spend time with all of them, Davina did not have the desire or energy to be the one to encourage Charlotte to change.

Winter eased its grip on the land, and the thaw slowly began. However, any joy with the change in the season was rapidly replaced when Davina realized it merely meant mud season had arrived. No matter how diligently she worked, the men tracked mud in everywhere.

"What has you in such a foul mood, Dav?" Slims asked, as he slipped into the big house's kitchen one midafternoon in the first weeks of March, and she glowered at him.

"That floor was spotless, aye?" she said, pointing to the kitchen floor and the muddy boot steps now marring them. "Do ye never consider I'm sick of washin' the *bluidy* floor?"

Slims looked from her scowl to the floor and back again, wisely opting for the correct option of a nod. "I'm sorry, love," he said, wrapping his arms around her waist and kissing her neck. "We wipe them down as best we can. I'll think of a solution." After kissing her again, he winked at her and returned to the barn to help Frederick, as he prepared for another of his mares to foal.

That evening, Davina paused at the entrance to the kitchen to find every ranch hand bootless in the kitchen. Slims grinned and winked at her, as she gaped at him.

"I told you that I'd think of a solution," he said proudly. "Although you might find our stinky feet more of a bother than any dirty floor."

Davina burst out laughing. "Oh, ye are too clever for yer own good." She stroked a hand down his arm and moved to the stove to lift a heavy casserole. She frowned at her husband when he gently pushed her aside.

"No, love, let me," he whispered, wrapping his hands in cloths and lifting the heavy pan. After setting it on small bricks on the table, he lifted off its lid and placed it nearby on the stove.

She watched him with an intrigued smile, biting her lip as she watched him interact and laugh with the men. Soon she knew more help would arrive, and they would be expected to eat with the men in the bunkhouse or alone in their cabin. For now, she stored up each memory, relishing each moment with her family and friends, wishing this idyllic time never had to end.

~

"Sorcha," Davina said a few days later. When her cousin looked up from working on a quilt that she planned to sell at Annabelle's store, Davina fidgeted in her chair. "I've been meanin' to show ye something, but I dinna want to cause trouble."

Sorcha set aside the quilt and focused fully on her cousin. "What do ye mean? Ye will no' cause trouble, Dav."

Davina smiled at the nickname everyone had picked up from Slims. "I'm not a fan of letters," she whispered. "You saw what happened to Slims and me after the arrival of that letter from my da." After a deep breath, she pulled a small packet of letters from her pocket. "I brought these with me because I thought I'd have to prove who I was. That ye'd never believe my story if I didna have some proof."

Sorcha's gaze lit with interest that she didn't attempt to conceal. "Letters?" she whispered. "Who wrote them?"

"My da has an odd habit of copying important letters he sends, in case there are ever disputes as to what he wrote. When I riffled through my da's papers, discovering you had not died along with Auntie Mairi, I found a few letters. One from my uncle, tellin' my da where you planned to move. 'Tis how I kent where to travel to. I also found letters my da had written. An' one from yer da."

"My da?" Sorcha asked, her eyes round. Her hand reached out, as though to snatch them from Davina. "Forgive me," she whispered. "I should no' take what is no' offered."

Davina smiled. "Nae, I offer them to ye, Sorcha, but ye must ken, my da is cruel. I dinna want to cause ye pain."

Sorcha nodded. "But my da is no'. Was no'. He was a good

man." She searched Davina's gaze, as though hoping to see agreement in her cousin's gaze.

"I never met him, but what I read in his letters shows him to be exceptional." She took a deep breath and handed the packet to her cousin. "I'll leave ye to read." Davina paused at the door, watching as her cousin traced over her father's handwriting as Ewan had. After a moment, she slipped out and then walked with purposeful strides down the hall and outside.

She pulled open the barn door, waiting a moment as her eyes adjusted to the darkened interior. She moved in the direction of a large stall where all the men stood, watching a horse inside. "Excuse me," she said, flushing as they all spun to stare at her. "Frederick, might I have a word."

Frederick nodded and approached. "It's not the best time, Davina. One of my mares is to foal soon."

"Oh." She hesitated before blurting out, "I gave Sorcha a packet of letters from Scotland. I fear they might upset her."

Frederick took off at a run, bellowing for Slims to come and get him, if needed.

Slims ambled to his wife, a curious expression warring with concern. "What's wrong?" He stared at the barn door. "What did you say to Fred?"

She shook her head, squeezing his hand. "Trust me," she whispered. When he nodded and didn't ask her any more questions, a doubt she didn't know she carried lifted. "What are ye starin' at?"

He winked at her and led her to the stall, standing behind her. She leaned against his strong chest, and he rested his chin on her head. "One of our fillies is about to have a baby. A foal."

"Oh, how precious," she whispered. She looked up at him. "Can I stay with ye an' watch?"

Tracing a finger down her cheek, he nodded. "Yes,

although you should know, it could take hours. For some reason, they like to have their foals in the middle of the night."

Davina turned around to stare at the beautiful horse. "She probably hopes ye'll lose interest an' give her a wee bit of privacy."

He laughed, tugging her close, as he wrapped an arm around her waist. "Aye, you're probably right," he whispered in her ear. "Anytime you want to go back to the cabin, let me know."

❧

F rederick burst into his wife's private sanctuary, gasping for breath and swearing softly at the sight of tears coursing down her cheeks. "Love?" he whispered.

She raised eyes filled with wonder and delight to meet his. "Oh, Frederick," she gasped. "Ye dinna ken what receivin' my da's letters means," she whispered, holding it out to him. "Davina's da is a miserable man, but my da, … my da," she whispered, as tears choked her throat, and she was unable to say anything more.

"Hush, love," he murmured, as he wrapped an arm around her shoulder. When she handed the old letters to him, yellowed with time, he read them slowly.

M *y Darling Mairi,*

May 23, 1859

I count the days until I can see you again. Your smile, your laughter, your radiant expression of your love for me fills me with a joy I never knew I could feel. I hear a song that you sing, and I remember being in your arms, as you serenaded me. I feel the sunshine on my face as I work the croft, and I feel your soft fingers stroking over me.

I do not deserve you, Mairi. I do not deserve a woman as honorable and as pure of spirit as you are. But I give thanks every day that you love me as I love you.

Although it will be months before I have reason to return to Portree, know that you are in my heart, and I count the hours until I can hold you in my arms again.

Yours forever,
Malcolm

~

D ear Mr. MacKinnon,

Sept 2, 1861

It is with the deepest shame that I find myself forced to write you, a dishonorable blackguard who would degrade the fine name and memory of my beloved sister, Mairi. How you ever inveigled yourself into her good graces, I will never understand. Mairi was always the most proper, well behaved of my siblings, and to know she fell so low brings me the greatest grief imaginable. To no longer consider her family due to her wickedness only engenders an even greater sorrow. To know she will not be interred in our family's plot will forever bring me grief.

Mairi died due to her wicked liaison with you, sir. If you had left her alone, she would never have come to such a sad death. Her child, your sinful spawn, will know what it is to suffer for the sins of her mother. She is not a MacQueen, nor will any of us ever accept her as one.

I pray every night that you do not have the effrontery to harm another innocent as you harmed Mairi.

Baldwin MacQueen

~

D*ear Mr. MacQueen,*

September 9, 1861

I find I must give you reluctant thanks for writing me about the death of my beloved Mairi. I had no idea she ailed nor that she was to give birth to my beloved daughter, Sorcha. Yes, Sorcha. Although you would have consigned my daughter to the living hell of being raised in an orphanage, she is now with me. She has the full protection of the MacKinnon name and is acknowledged as my daughter.

She will only ever know love. She will only ever know that she is cherished. For she is as precious to me as my sons.

Shame on you, Baldwin. She was your last living link to your sister, and you discarded her as though she were nothing more than a piece of rubbish. She's a living, breathing treasure, and 'tis your shame you will never have the opportunity to watch her grow. You'll never have the chance to see pieces of Mairi in her. If there is any justice in this world, she'll never know about you and your treatment of her, for I want her to never doubt how much she is loved and wanted.

Malcolm MacKinnon

F rederick let out a stuttering breath at the last line of his father-in-law's letter. "Oh, love," he whispered. "Now you will never doubt. It's here for you to read over and over again. From the moment you were born, you were treasured. Never doubt."

She threw herself in Frederick's arms. "I should no' need a letter. I should remember his carin' of me. His love of me."

184

She shuddered. "But he was always sad when he looked at me, an' I did no' understand. I ken now it was because he saw Mairi, an' he was missing her."

"Yes," he whispered. "No man can recover after loving a woman like you and losing her." His eyes glowed with a fervent hope. "I pray I never have to know such a fate."

"Hush," she murmured. "None of that talk." Sorcha rested her head on Frederick's shoulder. "Davina's da was cruel, aye?"

"Aye," Frederick murmured. "I wonder how much worse his letter was that he wrote your cousin."

Sorcha let out a deep breath, snuggling farther into his lap. "Davina was generous enough to bring me a letter, proving how much I was loved. How much my parents loved each other. I canna imagine the heartbreak of receivin' a letter from my da while he lived where he told me that he loathed me. That I was such a disappointment that he told neighbors and friends I was dead to him."

Frederick leaned back, cupping her face in his hands. "Her father said that?" When she nodded, Frederick groaned. "No wonder she reacted as she did, pushing Slims away."

"Aye," Sorcha murmured. "An' I ken 'twill take more than a few sweet words to take away the sting of a parent's rejection."

Frederick held her close to comfort her, as she fought to forget the woman who had raised her and had loathed her, instead murmuring words in her ear, encouraging her to focus on her real mother. The woman who had loved her but had died too soon.

∽

Hours later, Slims, Shorty, and Frederick sipped cups of coffee and chatted quietly as they watched the dark gray filly, Witching Hour, stomp and pace and grunt as she prepared to have her foal. Slims looked over his shoulder, smiling to see Davina wrapped up in a blanket, asleep on a soft pile of fresh hay. As Frederick eased into the pen to help the filly, if needed, Slims approached Davina.

"Darlin'," he whispered, as he ran a gentle hand over her head and arm. "It's time."

She woke with a start, a smile spreading at the sight of Slims. "Simon," she breathed. She arched up, kissing him softly. "Time for what?" she asked with a groan, as she tried to fully wake up.

"Time to watch Witching Hour have her foal." He grinned as she gave a small chirp of excitement, grabbing his arm for him to haul her upright.

She stepped forward, wrapping her arms around his chest for a moment, breathing in his scent of sweat, hay, and horse.

"I stink, Dav," he murmured, attempting to push her away from him. "I need to wash."

Gripping his hand, Davina pulled him in the direction of Shorty, Dalton, and Dixon. "No, ye smell like my husband, the most enticin' scent I've ever smelled." She winked at him as he gaped at her, turning to pay attention to Frederick and the filly. She giggled as he wrapped his arms around her, hauling her back against his front. Together, they watched the mare ably deliver her foal, and the foal's wobbly attempt to stand.

"Oh, how precious," Davina murmured. She looked over her shoulder at Slims with a look of wonder and awe. "Can I visit every day?"

He chuckled before kissing her cheek. "Of course you can, darlin'. Witchin' Hour's friendly, although she'll be a little cautious now that she has a young'un." His hands held her just a little tighter against him. "You live here. You can come and go as you want, Dav, unless there's a worry you'll be harmed."

"Thank you," she whispered, her gaze ensnared by watching the filly and the foal interact. "I feel like I could watch them forever." She smiled her thanks as Dalton handed her a steaming cup of coffee, and she turned to watch the foal thrust its head and attempt to figure out life outside of its mother's womb. He appeared black, but Davina suspected the foal would be a dark gray, like his mother. On his right flank, he had a jerky line. "Can I name him Lightning?"

Slims shook his head. "No, darlin'. A horse named Lightnin' is already in town. Bears's favorite horse."

She bit her lip a moment as she continued to watch the filly and the foal with an endless fascination. "Flash?" She smiled at Frederick as she saw him listening in to their conversation. At his nod, she gave a soft squeal of delight. "Oh, look at her," she breathed, as she watched Witching Hour ignore all of them, as she tended to Flash. "How many foals has she had?"

"This is her first," Slims murmured. "Fred was worried about her, but she did well."

"Aye, she did. I'll pray that her foal has continued health."

"Oh, Dav," her husband murmured, as he heard the sorrow in her voice.

With a bright smile, she handed the half-filled mug to Dalton and faced her husband. "Dinna mind me. I'm tired is all." She stroked a hand down Slims's strong arm. "I'm goin' to sleep for a few hours."

Frederick called out from inside the birthing stall, "Don't worry about breakfast tomorrow. Get plenty of rest, Davina."

Davina waved, marching for the door to her cabin. When

she was inside, she washed with cold water and then slipped into a flannel nightgown, before sliding under the blankets into the cold sheets. With a groan, she sat up, glaring at the stove, as she had forgotten to stoke the fire within. Sighing, she heaved the pile of blankets off her and rose to build up the fire. Once she was nestled in bed again, she attempted to force herself to sleep, but her mind wouldn't settle.

Over and over, she remembered the birth of her children. The horrible pain forgotten, instead recalling the over-whelming elation as they cried and then suckled at her breast. The wonder as she counted their fingers and toes. The amazement that any hair could be as silky and soft as a baby's downy head. The awe that she had created such a beautiful being.

Turning on her side, she attempted to focus on the joyous days she'd had with her babes, rather than the agonizing weeks, months, and years after she had lost them. Curling into as tight a ball as possible, she tried to prevent the pain from permeating the happiness of her present. However, she was discovering the past always had a way of oozing its way into the here and now. She worried she couldn't prevent the past from affecting her future.

She jumped, stifling a shriek, when a hand stroked her back. "Simon?"

"Were you expecting someone else?" he whispered.

She rolled over, grabbing his hand. "Of course no', dinna be foolish."

He frowned as he saw her expression. "Are you well, Davina?"

She reached out for him, as she scooted back in the bed. "Hold me, Simon," she said, a desperation in her gaze. "I need yer comfort just now."

He kicked off his boots and shed his clothes, crawling

into bed beside her. "*Shh*, love," he murmured. "Whatever it is, you're well. You're safe."

She shivered at his words, clinging to him.

His fingers played over her back, stroking a random pattern over the soft fabric of the flannel and through her hair. "I imagine tonight had you thinkin' about your babes," he said in a soft voice. When she pressed her face against his chest, he kissed her head. "I'm sorry you aren't holdin' them in your arms, Davina. That they aren't racin' around you, chattering away and raisin' havoc."

Her shoulders heaved as she sobbed into his chest. He held her close, rocking her as she cried. "I hate that I was such a failure," she stuttered out.

"*Shh*, love," he whispered. "You weren't then, and you aren't now." He lifted her chin so he could look into her tear-brightened eyes. "Your babes died. At no fault of yours."

He waited for her to protest his words, but she remained quiet. "What did the doctor say when he visited?"

"That they had weak lungs," she whispered. "There was nothin' to do for them. They never breathed well."

"But they were well loved," he said in a voice that brooked no doubt.

"Aye, oh aye."

"I'd take this pain for you if I could, but I can't."

Davina stared at him in wonder, as she turned her face into his thumb as it traced along her cheek, brushing away a tear. "How are ye so good to me?"

His eyes glowed with emotions. "You are cherished, Davina. Never forget that." He kissed her head, sighing with contentment as she rested her head on his chest, giving comfort and receiving it from her in equal measure.

CHAPTER 10

April entered with a thunderclap and seemed determined to continue as it began. The weather matched Davina's mood, for she was crotchety on the best of days, although she didn't know why. Men had begun to arrive at the ranch, looking for employment, and Charlotte had insisted she work as the cook for the men in the bunkhouse, ignoring Frederick's protestations that he preferred for her to remain in the big house. Davina missed the meals with Shorty, Dalton, and Dixon, who now ate all their meals in the bunkhouse. Slims and she ate with Sorcha and Frederick in the big house, although Slims would be absent a few nights a week to spend time with his men.

On an evening Slims had decided to tell tall tales and to play poker with the men, Davina sat in their cabin, sewing and listening to the rain *ping* off their roof. The sound was familiar and soothing, as it reminded her of home. Of Scotland. She shook her head as she realized home was here. With Slims. She couldn't imagine not having him in her life. How could she live away from the man she loved?

She gasped as the needle jabbed the tender flesh of her

finger at the word "love." She stared at the stove, her heart racing and pounding at the thought she could love him. Closing her eyes, she tried to think rationally. Instead all she could see was Slims. Always treating her well and with tender care.

Davina envisioned telling him how she felt, and a tidal wave of fear crashed over her. Shaking, she set down her needlework, as she knew she would only do herself more harm. This was one of her greatest fears, come to life. Loving and having that love rejected. It's why she'd told Sorcha that she had only ever cared for someone. She couldn't bear loving and not having that feeling reciprocated. Not again. With a stuttering sigh, she took a deep breath in an attempt to calm her roiling emotions.

As she relaxed, her mind envisioned Slims being delighted at the news. Her breath caught at such a possibility. "Am I brave enough to risk telling him?" she whispered to herself. Sitting in silence for long minutes, an inner battle raged over what she yearned to do and what she knew was safe.

She gasped as the door opened, and she stuck her finger in her mouth as though she had just stabbed it. Any courage she had mustered scattered like tumbleweeds in the wind at his presence.

"Dav?" Slims asked with a curious expression. "Are you well?"

"Aye," she said, as she extracted her finger to study it. "I poked my finger sewin'."

He chuckled. "A risk you have to take to continue to create such beautiful dresses, I'd think." He kissed her head and sighed with pleasure to sit beside her.

"Ye think my dresses fetchin'?" she asked.

"Aye, but perhaps it's simply because you're in them," he

said with a teasing glint in his gaze. He frowned when she failed to tease him back. "Are you well, Dav?"

"Aye," she said, rising to turn to the bed. "A wee bit tired."

"Tired?" he murmured, as he stood too. "Or attemptin' to avoid me?"

She cupped his cheek, an affectionate smile blooming as she stared at him. "Tired," she breathed, as she stood on her toes. "But never too tired for you."

He chuckled but stared at her. His fingers traced under her eyes, and he shook his head. "No, love," he whispered. "I can see you speak the truth. You're exhausted. Let me hold you while you sleep."

She pressed forward, wrapping her arms around him. "Yes, for I'll never rest well if you are far from me."

~

Slims traced butterfly-soft caresses over Davina's shoulders as she slumbered against him. Unlike his wife, who had tumbled into a deep sleep almost from the moment she laid down in bed, he had slept in fits and starts. Unable to fully relax, Slims noted a fine tension coiled through him, and he knew the reason. However, he feared he was a fool to consider upsetting the peace and harmony in his marriage. Was the dream of something even better worth the risk?

Davina stirred in his arms, and he kissed her head. "Mornin', my darling," he murmured. She snuggled close with a contented sigh, rubbing her face against his chest. He ran his fingers over her back a few more times, before he slipped from underneath her to move to the stove.

"Simon?" she whispered. "Why won't you stay in bed a little longer with me?"

He filled the kettle to boil water for coffee and stood with his back to her. "I ... Not today, Dav," he rasped.

She sat up with the blankets pooled around her waist, suddenly alert and staring at him with trepidation in her gaze. "Have I done somethin' to disappoint ye?" When he swore softly under his breath, she whispered, "To upset ye?"

"No, of course not," he snapped. He looked over his shoulder and took a calming breath when he saw her flinch at his tone.

"What is it?" she whispered.

He faced her, pulling the chair close, so he could sit at eye level with her, his gaze wild and filled with a mixture of dread and hope. "I fear I'm being a fool. Wishin' for more than I should."

Staring at him in complete befuddlement and then horror, Davina paled. "I told ye that ye'd want more from me."

"No," Slims said, gripping her hand. "I don't mean children, Dav." He closed his eyes and rubbed at his forehead with his free hand. "I'm mucking this up." He took a deep breath and forced himself to gaze deeply into her eyes. "Why are you happy with me? Why me and not another man?"

She sat back, as though affronted by the question, her hand slipping free of his. "How can ye ask me such a question?" She shook her head. "You're good an' kind an' honorable." She stared at him in confusion. "I didna think ye'd need such praise."

"No, Dav, what do you *feel* for me?" His brown eyes glowed with fervent passion.

"Feel for ye?" She swallowed and then shrugged, her shoulders turning down, as though needing to protect herself. "Ye ken I care for ye." She shrugged, her hands gripping the quilt in her agitation. "That I'm happy with ye."

"*Care* for me," he muttered in disgust. Slims sat for a long moment, the passion in his gaze fading to one of disillusionment. "You'll never tell me how you truly feel, will you?"

Slims murmured. "No matter what I do or what I say, nothing will ever be enough." He rose and pivoted to the door, stilling when he heard words that sounded as though they had been wrenched from her soul. "What?" he whispered.

She sat, crouched over herself on the unmade bed, with silent tears coursing down her cheeks.

He moved to the bed and knelt in front of her, his large hands kneading through her hair as he tangled the strands even further. "Tell me," he pleaded. "Tell me that I heard right. You love me?" His deep voice was filled with a youthful hopefulness.

"No," she moaned, as she covered her face, smearing her tears.

"You don't," he breathed, his hands falling from her, as it felt as though his heart stilled at the single word. In that instant, he understood what hell was: loving a woman who would never love him with an equal fervor.

"I'm sorry," she murmured.

He stood with alacrity, moving to stand as far away from her as possible in the cabin. "Sorry?" he spat out. "Sorry you can't feel anythin' more for me than lust?" He stood with his back turned toward her, his shoulders taut, as though recovering from a body blow, and did not see the arrested look on Davina's face. "Fool," he swore at himself.

"I didna mean to ..." Her shoulders heaved as she fought a sob. "I didna mean to ruin everythin' between us by sayin' it too soon." She waited for some response from him, but he seemed to not have heard her whispered admission.

Davina pushed herself to stand, approaching him on wobbly legs. When she stood within an arm's length, she reached out a quivering hand to stroke down his back. "Slims," she whispered. "Simon."

"Don't call me that. Not when ... Not now," he rasped

out. He listened intently with head bowed, expecting to hear her soft footsteps as she retreated and then left their cabin. Instead, he imagined he could feel her subtle warmth behind him. Like a fool, his body swayed backward, yearning to be closer to her. "Don't torture me like this," he pleaded.

"Forgive me," she whispered, her voice calmer and clearer.

"It's not your fault you can't esteem a man like me. How could a woman as fine as you ever respect a man who was a coward? A man who ran off, rather than fought for his heritage?"

"Simon," she breathed. "Ye are no' a coward. Ye would have been killed, an' then none would have remembered and honored yer family. Ye lived, as ye ken yer mother and da would have wanted ye to. There is no shame in that."

He sighed, his back still to her. "I was a fool to believe you'd ever esteem me, Dav. I'm just a cowpoke." When she jabbed him in his shoulder with a finger, he grunted and spun to glare at her.

"I dinna ever want to hear ye call yerself that again. Ye're so much more than a ... a ... cowpoke." She paused as her voice tumbled over the unfamiliar word. "Ye're magnificent." Stepping up to him, she held out her quivering hands to cup his face. "I didna mean I was sorry for lovin' ye." She stared at him with wonder, as a tear sparkled on one cheek. "How could I ever regret that?"

He shook his head, his hands at his side, as he stared at her with longing and bewilderment. "Davina, I don't understand. You were sobbing."

She pelted him on his chest, the soft slap feeling like the thump of a hummingbird's wing against his strong chest. "I wanted ye to tell me first!" she yelled. In a calmer voice, she said, "No one but my aunt Mairi has ever loved me, and I'm terrified of lovin' and no' being loved in return. I wanted to ken ye felt the same." She flushed as she admitted her fear.

"How do you feel?" he asked. When she stared at him in mute defiance, he sighed. "You daft woman," he murmured, using a word he'd learned from her cousin, Sorcha. With a wry, almost amused quirk of his lips, he relented.

Her breath caught at the startling depth of emotions in his unguarded gaze. She took a step closer to him, her hands gripping his strong arms, as though anchoring her in place.

"How can you not understand how much I love you?" He stared deeply into her eyes. "I adore you. I cherish you. The thought of you ever suffering any harm torments me." Lowering his forehead to rest against hers, he closed his eyes. "The mere thought that an uncharitable word could cause you pain enrages me. I'd go mad if anyone hurt you."

She took a step back, gazing deeply into his eyes. She blurted out, "But I'm not worth such concern."

His eyes blazed with anger at her disparaging words about herself. "You are, my love. You are." He lowered his head, his lips teasing hers for a fleeting moment before he deepened the kiss. With a deep sigh and a moan of regret, he forced himself to take a step back and to gaze with ardent devotion into her gaze. "I love you, Davina. I'll always be thankful Frederick insisted I take you to town that day."

Her smile bloomed, her fingers rubbing over his whiskers. "I love ye, Simon. More than I could ever say." She raised her fingers to cover his lips. "I feared ye didna feel as I did, an' I was terrified of bein' in another lopsided marriage. I dinna think I could survive that again."

"Oh, it's lopsided," he said, as he tugged her into his arms and swung her around, laughing as she squealed. He laid her down on the bed, his hands roving over her reverently. "It's impossible you could love me with the same ferocity I feel for you."

"No, 'tisn't," she protested, arching up to kiss him. "Come here, an' I'll prove it to ye."

～

A few days later, Davina entered the horse barn after Dalton had given her a message she was needed there. Although she was in the middle of baking bread, she set aside her apron, washed her hands, and hurried to the barn. Upon entering, she looked around, her alert gaze searching for trouble. She paused at Witching Hour's stall, her anxiety dropping to see Flash healthy and staring at her with mild curiosity.

"Dav," Slims said with warm humor. "Come with me." He held out his hand, his warm palm enveloping hers, as he led her away from the foal.

"Why am I here? I have bread rising, Simon."

He chuckled, pausing to brush at her cheeks. "I can surmise," he murmured. "You're covered in flour." He sobered as he stared deeply into her eyes. "I've asked Miss Sorcha to help with the cookin' today."

When she gaped at him, he flushed. "I know it isn't proper of me to ask her to do your work, but I wanted time with you, and we'll be busy soon. She didn't mind."

"I dinna understand," Davina whispered.

He stared at her tenderly. "Do you think I don't notice your interest in the horses? I think your love for them is only rivaled by Frederick's." His smile softened as she flushed. "And yet you've never asked to spend any time with them. I hoped you'd want to go on a ride with me today."

"A ride?" she gasped, her gaze filled with wonder. Taking a step closer to him, she gazed at him with a near reverence. "Truly?"

He smiled. "Yes, although I don't know if I could bear to

see you galloping around. I fear it will be a slow amble across the fields."

She gave a shriek of delight, throwing herself into his arms. A horse nickered in reproof at the noise, and she giggled. "Oh, thank ye, Simon. Thank ye."

He swung her around once before kissing her softly. "Come. Let's ride." After helping her onto Scout, a beautiful chestnut filly with a white chest, he mounted Pirate, a huge black stallion.

Soon they were on the range, with green grass shooting up all around them. In the distance were scattered cattle, eagerly eating the fresh vegetation. Walking the horses at a steady pace, the ranch house was quickly out of sight.

Pausing, Davina stared in wonder at the vast expanse of open land all around her. The mountains rose in the distance, providing a sharp border to the otherwise never-ending vista. "I never imagined such a place existed," she breathed. Closing her eyes, she took another deep breath, inhaling the fresh scent of the loamy earth. Smiling, she murmured, "I never realized the birdsong would be so different from Scotland."

He urged Pirate a little closer to Scout. "I imagine everything is different."

She smiled at him. "Aye," she whispered, as she leaned over to one side of her saddle in an attempt to kiss him. She squealed as she almost toppled out, but he caught her and tilted toward her to kiss her gently. "I've never ridden astride before. Feels a bit darin'."

He chuckled. "Well, we aren't fancy here, Dav. And there's never been a reason for a sidesaddle at the ranch." He caressed her cheek, before easing back into his saddle and gripping the pommel with both hands. "I'd prefer if you only rode out with me."

"As long as ye promise I dinna have to wait until next

April when ye're no' busy again." At his nod and smile of relief at her agreement, she closed her eyes again, as though listening. "What do ye call those birds that are singin'?"

He stilled, attuned to her interest in the world around her. "A finch. A meadowlark. A robin." He opened his eyes and smiled at her as she frowned, as though attempting to match the call to the bird.

"What's that rattling cry?" she murmured.

"I think the cranes have returned," he said with a smile. "That's what they sound like when they call out while flying." He motioned to her. "Come. Let's see if we can find some."

After a few hours of riding along the fields with no cranes in sight, he sighed. "Well, it was worth a try. They are a majestic bird." He gazed at her adoringly. "Would you like a rest?"

"Aye," Davina said. "Although I dinna ken how I'll manage to get off this gentle beast."

He chuckled as he dismounted and tied his reins to a nearby willow branch. Goldfinches and sparrows swooped overhead, while the striking black-and-white magpies watched the interlopers with mild interest from their high perch. "That's the benefit of having married a giant of a husband. I can help you." He lifted her off with ease, cradling her against his chest for a few moments before settling her on the ground. "All right?"

"I think I need to stay here a while," she breathed. "I've lost all strength in my legs."

He held her close until she pushed away from him to explore the small creek running nearby. After extracting a blanket and food from his saddlebags, he set up a small picnic in the shade of the willows. After she returned from her exploration with damp face, neck, and hands, he held out his arms. "What do you think?"

"I think I married a brilliant man," she said, as she

wrapped her arms around his neck. "Thank ye for such a perfect day, Simon."

He held her close, breathing in her subtle scent. "I needed this as much as you did."

"Perhaps," she whispered, looking up to meet his gaze, tears glistening in her eyes. "But ye listened and paid attention. Ye did no' reject my fascination with horses as a folly, an' I thank ye."

"Folly?" he asked with a shake of his head. "If given the chance, I suspect you could be a partner to Frederick." He held her head, refusing to allow her to duck away out of embarrassment or modesty. "You are bright, Dav, and passionate. I hate to think you'd toil away in a kitchen when your true love was in a stable."

She bit her lip and smiled at him. "Aye, my true love *is* in a stable."

His adoring gaze met hers, as he squeezed her waist. "You know what I meant."

Nodding, she whispered, "Aye. But I dinna ken anything about horses. I like them. I've always wanted to be around them, but I dinna ken anything useful."

"I know you, Dav, and I know you can learn. I know you can do whatever you want."

Staring at him with trepidation in her gaze, she asked in a low voice, "An' ye would no' resent the time I spent focused on horses?"

"Resent?" he whispered. "Hell no." He flushed after swearing. "If it makes you happy, Dav, it will make me happy. It's as simple as that."

"Oh, Simon," she breathed, pressing into his chest. "How I love you."

❧

I n late April, Davina stood at the paddock fence, watching as Slims and the men prepared for the spring roundup. She watched as Slims organized the men and the supplies they would need for the branding, although her gaze darted to Dalton, who seemed to hover near Charlotte. Whenever Charlotte needed help stocking the improvised chuck wagon, Dalton appeared at her elbow, eager to help. Davina hoped she remembered to speak with Slims about any potential relationship between Dalton and the woman she still didn't fully trust.

Although Charlotte had emerged from her sickroom and had insisted on working as a cook for the men in the bunkhouse, a miasma of despair clung to her. She had refused every overture of friendship from Davina and Sorcha. Davina suspected Charlotte had attempted to repulse any aid from Dalton too. However, Dalton appeared undeterred in his desire to help Charlotte and to keep any of the new ranch hands at bay. Although Davina wanted Dalton to find love, she feared Charlotte would only bring him more heartbreak.

Slims had spoken with Frederick about Davina helping with the horses, and Frederick was eager for her to learn as much as possible. She now had a stack of books in the cabin to read during her free time, to study, and to learn all she could about horses. She had also discovered that Slims had sent away for more books for her, but she wouldn't ruin his surprise when they arrived. After the roundup, he had also arranged for them to be away from the ranch for a few days, so she could spend time with Bears at the livery. With a contented sigh, she stared at the man who ensured her dreams came true, her heart overflowing with love for him.

Davina smiled at Irene, who had insisted she and Harold close the café to join in on the roundup, and Davina stood in quiet companionship with the older woman for a few moments. A robin trilled; a gentle breeze blew, and the promise of a successful roundup was in the air.

"Are you well, my girl?" Irene asked as she wrapped an arm around Davina's shoulders.

"Yes, missus, verra well," she whispered. "Although I hate no' bein' useful."

Irene laughed. "Don't worry. If the roundup goes well, the men will throw an impromptu hoe down, and you'll dance so much that you'll think your legs will fall off."

Davina paled at the prospect, leaning into Irene's side. "I'm no' one for dancin'."

"Tell that to your husband," Irene suggested with a chuckle, as she watched Slims lead the men. "He'll ensure you only do what you want. And I'd suggest you sing as a way to compensate for disappointing the men."

Davina nodded. "Thank ye, Irene. Ye are always so kind to me."

Irene pivoted slightly, so she could look at Davina. "And why shouldn't I be?" When Davina stared at her wide-eyed, Irene smiled at her with a loving look in her gaze. "All will be well, Davina. Slims is a good man."

Davina raised her eyebrows, her eyes widening. "I ken he is, Irene. I love him."

Grinning with satisfaction, Irene pulled her close. "Oh, my dear girl, I'm so glad. You have no idea how long I've hoped and prayed for a woman just like you to come into his life. He's needed you for so long."

Davina sniffled, fighting tears. "Aye, I ken. Just as I've needed him."

"Did you know that," Irene asked, "when I first met Slims, I feared he would never trust anyone again?" She nodded when Davina gaped at her in wide-eyed wonder. "I feared he would always look upon everything Harold, the boys, or I did with suspicion. Only with time, and constancy, did he come to realize we were good, honest people."

"Thank ye for carin' for him when he lost everythin'," Davina whispered.

Irene leaned forward and spoke in a low voice, as though imparting a secret. "As I'm sure you discovered, he wasn't hard to love."

Davina let out a stuttering breath, her gaze unerringly finding her husband, patiently talking to one of the new hands. "Nae. He's far too easy to love."

"Come," Irene said, slipping her arm through Davina's and leading her toward the big house. "Let's find Sorcha and talk about what we'll bring with us. Tomorrow will come soon enough, with us trundling along in a rickety wagon. Be thankful we won't have far to go."

Davina listened with rapt interest as Irene regaled her with tales of the long wagon journey from Fort Benton when they had first moved to the valley of Bear Grass Springs, any concerns for tomorrow momentarily forgotten.

~

After a successful first day, fiddles emerged, feet stomped, and men sang. Sorcha danced with the men, while Frederick watched, with baby Harold in his arms. Slims stood beside him, with Mairi asleep against his shoulder, and Davina stared at her husband in wonder as he appeared perfectly at ease to hold the child and to carry on a conversation at the same time.

Shorty stepped up to her and offered his hand. "Oh, Shorty," she whispered as she flushed. "I'm no' dancin' tonight."

"Is it because you're savin' all your dances for your husband?" Shorty asked with a teasing smile.

"Nae," Davina said, as she shook her head at other men who approached. "I'm no' dancing with anyone."

Shorty followed her gaze and smiled at the sight of his boss and his best friend holding the two children. "They make a picture, don't they? Only thing better would be if Slims had his own child. I know he's given up the notion of havin' children, but he'd make a good pa. But he claims he's content playin' uncle."

Her breath caught at Shorty's words, and she was thankful the loud music and singing drowned out the need for her to reply.

"I mean no offense, missus," Shorty said, as he realized he could have inadvertently offended her.

She shook her head and forced a smile, watching as Slims handed Mairi to Sorcha, who took a break from the dancing. Shorty doffed his hat and slipped into the group of men.

After a few moments, Slims saw her and approached with a wide grin. He held out his hand to grab hers, so as to lead her onto the makeshift dance floor. She pulled at his hand, digging in her heels. "Nae, Slims, nae," she breathed. "I canna. I willna."

Stilling at the terror and fear in her gaze, he took a step closer, acting as a buffer from the high-strung men and the music. "Dav? What's the matter?"

She bit her lip and grabbed his hand, dragging him away from the small celebration, their way lit by the full moon. "I didna want to tell ye. I thought to wait to make sure." Her shoulders slumped. "I wish I could avoid the pain altogether."

Slims stilled her frantic march across the prairie, his worried gaze meeting her panicked one. "What in God's name is goin' on, Dav?" he demanded.

She trembled, her eyes filling with tears. "I didna think it would happen," she whispered. "I'm so sorry."

"What?" he asked, giving her a little shake. "Are you ill? Am I going to lose you?"

"Nae," she gasped out. "I'm with child." Tears coursed down her cheeks after she blurted out her news.

Slims stood stock-still for a few moments, the wind whispering around them and the howl of a distant wolf preventing him from thinking he was dreaming. "With my child?"

She hit him on his chest. "Of course 'tis yours." She shook her head in disgust. "As if I ever wanted another man to touch me." She stomped her foot in her agitation and then gasped out, "*Oof*," as Slims yanked her against him.

"Oh, my darling," he whispered, as an awed smile bloomed. "I never dared dream or hope this would occur. I've loved you enough times that I knew it was possible, but …" He broke off, his hand shaking, as it caressed her head. "Are you well? Do you need anything?"

She pushed forward, into his embrace. "I need to know my bairn willna die this time," she whispered against his chest. She took a deep breath, as though marshaling all her courage. "I need to ken ye willna see me as a failure if my bairn dies. That ye will no' take your love away because I failed again."

His eyes gleamed with a fierce intensity, filled with love and devotion. "Never, Dav. I am not the spineless idiot you first married. I love you. I will love you forever. With no children. Or with ten." He smiled at her tenderly. "Don't doubt me." His pleading-filled voice provoked a shiver.

"I try no' to," she said, "but 'tis hard not to worry about what will come, when the past reminds me of all the heartache I already suffered."

He brushed away a tear and murmured, "And it's *our* bairn, my love."

She smiled at him, her eyes filled with joy at his words and his devotion.

"Why wouldn't you dance?" he asked.

"What if the jumpin' around caused harm to the bairn? What if I did somethin' to cause it to be born weak?" she whispered.

"Oh, Dav," he groaned, hauling her into his arms. "We'll go to town. Talk with Helen. Have her answer all your questions and reassure you as best she can. And I'll hold you, whenever you need comforting. I'll never tire of showing you how much I treasure you." His hand dropped to her waist, and his voice shook. "Or the child you shelter." He dropped his head down, until he rested his forehead against hers. "Thank you, Dav," he whispered.

"For what?"

"For facing your worst fear," he said around his tears. "For facing them so that I might have my deepest dream."

She bit her lip, and he traced her lip with his thumb, preventing her from saying anything more.

"You are not a failure. You will never be a disappointment. You are a woman, *my* woman, doing her best, and I could never ask for more." He kissed her reverently, as he placed a hand on her belly. "You've given me everything I ever dreamed of and so much more. I'll prove your every dream true," he murmured, pulling her close. "I promise."

She shuddered, holding him close. "Ye already have, my Simon. Ye already have."

EPILOGUE

Mountain Bluebird Ranch, 1896

Davina held a hand up to her forehead, as she stared over the prairie, the early evening light casting a warm glow on all she beheld. Prairie grass rose tall, swaying in the gentle breeze, as the mountains in the distance took on a purplish hue. Her breath caught as a shriek carried on the wind, but, with a mother's instinct, she knew it was a shriek of joy rather than a call for help.

Slims continued to work as foreman at the ranch, while Davina split her time between caring for her children and working with Frederick's horses. Slims never begrudged her time doing the work she loved, and her children loved every moment they spent with their cousins while she was busy away from their home.

With a contented sigh, she leaned back into her husband's strong chest as he wrapped his arms around her middle, tugging her close. "How are you, my darlin'?" he murmured into her neck, kissing her softly.

"Happier than I ever thought I could be," she whispered, turning abruptly to bury her face against his chest.

"*Shh*, love," he murmured. "What's this?" He rubbed a hand up and down her back as she cried softly against him. "Have our blessed demons driven you mad today?"

Chuckling, Davina rested her cheek against his strong muscles, her hands now tracing patterns on his back, rather than clinging to him. "No. Today was another miracle. We played and painted. I began to teach wee Elise how to knit and Jasper to read while we worked. Then it was time to romp around outside, and they've been having fun for hours."

Slims kissed her head, his gaze lighting on his children, running and laughing in the distance. "Why the tears, my love?"

"They're so healthy," she whispered. "I stare at them and can't believe they are mine. Ours." She raised her face so her gaze met his. "I feel as though my heart will overflow."

His expression softened, as he stared deeply into her beautiful brown eyes. "Ah, lass, now you know how I've felt every moment since I met you." He kissed her softly. "And the wonder is, we have so many more yet to come."

~

Never fear! The Bear Grass Springs adventures continue. Healing Montana Love available in September 2020!

SNEAK PEEK AT HEALING MONTANA LOVE!

Mountain Bluebird Ranch, Montana Territory, May, 1889

Charlotte Ingram stood on the bunkhouse stoop at the Mountain Bluebird Ranch near the town of Bear Grass Springs, Montana. A meadowlark warbled and she gave thanks the breeze blew in the opposite direction today, sending the barn's stench away from the bunkhouse. Although she understood she should be thankful for the pungent odors, as it meant there was milk and butter and food to eat, she had yet to become accustomed to ranch life.

Although she had been on the ranch since February, the months seemed to crawl by. First because she was in a miasma of pain and despair. Now, because everyday consisted of a monotony of similar chores. She took a deep breath of the fresh air, closing her eyes with delight as she scented the faint hint of lilac on the breeze. Finally, spring was arriving. Wisps of reddish blond hair tickled her cheeks as they fluttered in the faint breeze, having escaped the braid down her back. Her sensible faded blue calico dress flapped at her ankles and she tugged her serviceable shawl around her shoulders.

With a sigh, she returned to the kitchen to prepare another meal for the men. Although they were courteous, few were overtly flirtatious and none crossed the line into impropriety. The men knew they would be fired and forced to find work on another less prosperous ranch if they harassed her. Saying a silent prayer of thanksgiving for men like Frederick Tompkins and his foreman, Slims, for ensuring she was respected, she hummed while she worked.

Soon, Charlotte was lost to her work, focusing on preparing a large apple crumble from the last of the previous year's crop while bread baked in the oven and stew bubbled on the stove. With a shriek, she spun and held a knife out as someone tapped her arm. "Stay away," she gasped.

Dalton held his hands up, his blue eyes rounded with surprise as he barely backed away in time to prevent a stabbing. The sound of his shirt tearing filled the otherwise silent room. "Miss Ingram," he murmured in a low voice. "I didn't mean to startle you. You were woolgathering." He shrugged as he took another step backward, his alert gaze on her as her arm quivered. "Why don't you put the knife down? No one will harm you here." He stood half a foot taller than her with long arms and could easily have manhandled the knife away from her. However, he did not attempt to touch her again.

In an instant, Charlotte flushed beet red and spun to face away from him. The muffled sound of her stifling a sob carried and he took a hesitant step in her direction. However, he couldn't see the knife and he had no desire for her aim to prove more accurate this time. "Miss Ingram?"

"Forgive me," she gasped out, her sherry-colored eyes filled with humiliation as she looked at him over her shoulder. "I was foolish. If you leave me your shirt, I'll mend it."

She bowed her head as she fought to control her quivering. The knife clattered to the countertop beside the stove.

He took a few ponderous steps, pulling out a chair with a loud scrape as though to indicate he were a fair distance away from her. "I wondered if there was any coffee left in the pot."

A hysterical laugh burst forth and she slammed her hand over her mouth to prevent any further inappropriate sounds from emerging. However, she knew she was on the verge of giving in to her fears, of never feeling secure, and she could not prevent the hot scald of tears as they poured down her cheeks.

"Miss?" He murmured, suddenly standing behind her again. At the soft touch to her shoulder, she flinched and then relaxed. "Miss, you're safe here. You know the men are loyal to you."

She refused to turn and face him. In a stuttering voice, she rasped, "No, they're loyal to the Missus. The two Missus. They tolerate me. And give me a wide berth because they don't want to lose their jobs." She took a long breath, finally corralling her out of control emotions. Reaching a shaking hand out, she grasped a coffee cup and filled it. "I believe you like it black."

She turned to hand it to him, refusing to meet his gaze.

"Look at me," he whispered. When she kept her eyes downcast, he murmured, "Please."

At the entreaty, her gaze flew to his and she frowned in confusion. Men gave her orders. They didn't make polite requests she could refuse. She met his worried gaze, his blue eyes with wrinkles at the corners as he focused all of his attention on her. His brown hair was scrunched down like he'd just taken his hat off, and she fought an irrational urge to run her hands through it.

"I know someone hurt you, Miss Ingram. It's plain to see.

213

But not all men are scoundrels." He paused as he reached forward to accept the cup of coffee from her. "One day, you'll come to realize you can trust more than yourself." With a nod of his head, he left.

Charlotte stood in frozen wonder for a long moment, wondering if she had imagined the entire interlude. *Interlude?* She asked herself as she berated herself for being fanciful. Her imagination was what had led to her near murder. With a shiver, she faced the stove again, determined to forget Dalton. To forget his solicitude. His kindness. His constancy. For she knew it was always a pretense to entice a woman to do something she might have had the sense to decline.

She took a deep breath to calm her nerves. Instead, his alluring scent teased her senses. Musky, with a hint of sandalwood cologne mixed with sweat and the scent of horses. With a huff, she turned to the window and took a gulp of the clean spring air, determined to ignore any and all attraction for a ranch hand named Dalton.

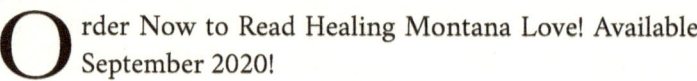

Order Now to Read Healing Montana Love! Available September 2020!

NEVER MISS A RAMONA FLIGHTNER UPDATE!

Thank you for reading *Lassoing a Montana Heart*! I hope you enjoyed it as much as I enjoyed writing it.

I love hearing from you, so please feel free to write me and let me know what you think!

You can reach me at: ramona@ramonaflightner.com

Join My Newsletter For Updates, and Sneak Peeks about the series you love!

Want new release alerts, access to bonus materials and exclusive giveaways, and all my announcements first? Subscribe to my weekly newsletter!

Want to be notified about freebies and sales? Try Bookbub!

Want to stay up to date on new releases, my life in beautiful Montana, and research trip adventures? Find Me On Facebook! Or Find Me On Instagram!

Unbridled Montana Passion (BGS, Book 7) Fidelia and Bears

Montana Vagabond (BGS, Book 8) Ben and Jane

Exultant Montana Christmas (BGS, Book 9) Ewan and Jessamine

Lassoing a Montana Heart (BGS, Book 10) Slims and Davina

Healing Montana Love (BGS, Book 11) Coming in September 2020!

Runaway Montana Groom (BGS Book 12) Coming Soon!

The Banished Saga

Follow the McLeod, Sullivan and Russell families as they find love, their loyalties are tested, and they overcome the challenges of their time. A sweeping saga set between Boston and Montana in early 1900's America. Finally, the Saga is complete!

The Banished Saga: (In Order)

Love's First Flames (Prequel)

Banished Love

Reclaimed Love

Undaunted Love (Part One)

Undaunted Love (Part Two)

Tenacious Love

Unrelenting Love

Escape To Love

Resilient Love

Abiding Love

Triumphant Love

ACKNOWLEDGMENTS

Writing is an act of love, but also of perseverance. Knowing that there are fans, eager to read the next book, makes sitting in a chair for hours as I think of ways for my characters to act is a gift. Thank you!

My family is patient with me as I continue to disappear to work on novels and research. Thank you for your ongoing interest and enthusiasm!

DB- you're the best! Your ability to catch little mistakes and your enthusiasm are invaluable. As is your friendship. Thank you!

Jenny Q- thank you for your patience with me as you continue to produce gorgeous covers.

ABOUT THE AUTHOR

Ramona is a historical romance author who loves to immerse herself in research as much as she loves writing. A native of Montana, every day she marvels that she gets to live in such a beautiful place. When she's not writing, her favorite pastimes are fly fishing the cool clear streams of a Montana river, hiking in the mountains, and spending time with family and friends.

Ramona's heroines are strong, resilient women, the type of women you'd love to have as your best friend. Her heroes are loyal and honorable, men you'd love to meet or bring home to introduce to your family for Sunday dinner. She hopes her stories bring the past alive and allow you to forget the outside world for a while.

BB bookbub.com/authors/ramona-flightner
⊙ instagram.com/rflightner
f facebook.com/authorramonaflightner
⑫ pinterest.com/Ramonaauthor

www.ingramcontent.com/pod-product-compliance
Lightning Source LLC
Chambersburg PA
CBHW022141240626
47153CB00007B/2460